D1596238

The
Dark
Ships

for Megan,

Best wishes

Tom Townsend
2-24.87

The Dark Ships

Tom Townsend

EAKIN PRESS
Austin, Texas

FIRST EDITION

Published in the United States of America
By Eakin Press, P.O. Box 23069, Austin Texas 78735

ISBN 0-89015-579-8

For Janet,
Forever my Lady . . . my love

Preface

This tale continues the adventures of Jem, but it is intended to do more than just probe deeper into his own mysterious past. We will again meet his ever practical and business-minded friend, Raif. Talva, daughter of the witch Lady Gray, is here too. And oh yes, so is that shadowy figure of the privateer, Jean Lafitte.

Nevertheless, *The Dark Ships* is a story within itself, with new villains and new dangers. There is also a new, and most unlikely, friend named Mariah.

This story may answer some questions which were only hinted at in *Where the Pirates Are*. But rest assured, there are new questions left to be answered in tales as yet untold.

1

Low in the eastern sky there was a full moon. It splashed the ocean with dancing phantoms of pale light as a steady rhythm of crashing surf echoed on the wind.

A ship crossed the moon and ghosted cautiously in toward Rollover Pass. She was a dark shadow, long and knifelike, with raked masts and a bowsprit which seemed as long as her masts were high. Only her jibs and topsails were set. She showed no light and flew no flag, but her gunports were open and moonlight reflected off the long muzzles of her cannon.

From the sand dunes of Bolivar Island, moonlight also caught the lens of a brass telescope as a group of shadowy figures watched her approach.

"It be the *Pride* all right," the man with the telescope announced in a rasping voice. "Now spread out ya lubbers, and keep down or you'll be collectin' no bounty on Ol' Black Jack tonight."

Shadows of a dozen men darted among the dunes. Cutlasses whispered from their sheaths, and the ominous cocking of muskets echoed quietly in the night.

The dark ship had turned into the wind and backed her sails. Canvas popped and cracked as she rocked nervously with her masts tracing a wide arc across the night sky. As the man with the telescope watched, a single longboat was lowered and began pulling toward the shore.

"I think they suspects somethin', Mr. Vibart," a little man beside him whispered.

The one called Vibart lowered his telescope and spit on the sand. "Lopez, ya lubber, you worry more than my old grandmother, may she rest in peace." He jerked his thumb in the direction of the ship. "With the price there be on his head, that old fox wouldn't come within sight of land without first clearing for action an' runnin' out his guns, all of 'em double charged with grapeshot."

Lopez did not answer but shifted uneasily as the longboat rode in over the breakers and grounded in the surf. Two figures splashed into the knee-deep water.

"Well, give 'em the signal now an' be quick about it," Vibart barked.

Lopez removed the shield from the lantern he carried and swung it back and forth three times above his head. A few nervous seconds passed before it was answered by a matching signal, and two men moved up the beach to meet them at the edge of the wet sand.

"Captain," Vibart greeted.

The man who answered was a faceless silhouette against the night sky. Vibart could tell that he wore high boots and a hat with the brim pinned up on one side. A sword hung at his side. Moonlight glinted for a second off the brass butts of a brace of pistols in his wide belt, but any other details were hidden beneath a heavy cloak.

"Magnus Vibart," the faceless shadow said in a voice as chilling as a December gale. "It has been a long time. And this I assume is Monsieur Lopez?"

Vibart's eyes strayed to the giant of a man who flanked the captain. He too was faceless in the night, but his very bulk seemed to blot out the southern sky. He carried a blunderbuss, a short, vicious gun which could tear a man in half at five paces.

"What news have you?" the captain asked. "I am getting too old for prowling about this coast late at night."

Vibrant found his tongue as he slipped the telescope into his pocket. "We've seen the likes of no Mexican ships hereabouts in many months."

"Nothing at all? One of my corsairs shadowed a frigate and a transport north from Vera Cruz only a few weeks past. I have been assured that they were bound for someplace in Texas."

Vibart shifted uneasily. "Perhaps they sailed east for New Orleans or Pensacola. They could have steered clear of these shores and — "

His sentence went unfinished as the giant with the blunderbuss spoke suddenly. Three yellow lanterns had been hoisted aloft in the dark ship's rigging. "*Pride's* signalin' Cap'n. Enemy in sight."

Even as the captain turned to face the sea, the giant was pointing at the far horizon. "Sail to the southwest."

"And to the east as well," the captain echoed.

Vibart's moment had come. The trap was about to spring. His hand reached the pistol hidden in his pocket as he nodded to Lopez and noticed sweat dripping on the small man's forehead.

His thumb was cocking the pistol's hammer when a sea gull rose suddenly from the dunes behind them. It squawked loudly and its wings beat the air as it soared up into the night sky.

Vibart cursed under his breath, certain that one of his men had stepped on it accidentally. But the damage was done. A single musket shot rang out from the dunes and the captain turned, his hand already on his sword. The weapon hissed from its scabbard, its ornate hilt catching Vibart's pistol just as it came out of his pocket.

"A bloody trap!" the giant warned as the pistol discharged into the sand and the heel of the captain's boot knocked Vibart to the ground. The night exploded as mu-

3

skets discharged and shots whined about them. The butt of the blunderbuss came down on Lopez's head with a hollow thud, and the little man dropped like an anchor.

The two men from the sea retreated toward the longboat as their attackers surged out from the dunes. The giant laughed as the blast from his blunderbuss belched a four-foot tongue of flame which turned night into day and cut down the closest three like so many stands of wheat.

The cold ring of steel against steel echoed along the beach as the attack was pressed in close to the longboat's bow. "Finish 'em, ya lubbers!" Vibart was shouting as he staggered to his feet and followed the fight. "Ye've got 'em now, finish 'em, finish 'em!" Vibart was still yelling, urging his men on to the kill when the captain and the giant suddenly ducked beside the longboat.

There followed a sudden, deadly moment of silence as Vibart's men stared dumbly at a swivel gun mounted in the longboat's bow. A portly figure stood behind it. They never saw his face in the night, but the slow match he held in his left hand glowed blood red.

"Farewell me hearties," he laughed, and the gun fired. Sixteen small iron balls along with a few ship's nails and the broken glass from two rum bottles blasted into the tightly grouped men and ended the attack as swiftly as it had begun. When the smoke cleared. Vibart and a few survivors were running for the dunes, but most lay in untidy piles on the beach.

"Nicely done, Fat Jack," the captain said, getting to his feet and nodding to the man in the longboat. "But I fear a bit too late." He pointed to sea. "The *Pride* has made sail without us, as rightly she had to."

"Aye, Cap'n Jean," Fat Jack agreed unhappily. "And one of the Mexicans is closin' fast. He'll put a party ashore and be after us within the hour."

The captain rubbed his gray mustache and was silent for a moment. His ship was already under way and setting all the sail she carried. One enemy warship was to the east, pressing hard to cut her off. Close along the western shore the other ship was moving in to land a party. Thunder rolled in the distance as one of the Mexican bowchasers was fired blindly into the night.

"Quite right, Fat Jack," he agreed, *"Pride* will return for us after she has led the Mexicans a merry chase. Don't you agree, Mr. Cochrane?" He indicated the big man who was now relieving one of the less fortunate attackers of pistols, powder, and shot. The giant only grunted and the captain added: "until then, we will have to fend for ourselves, but I still have a friend or two along this coast." He pointed at the longboat which had brought them ashore. "Put a round through her keel; I'll not leave the enemy a good boat."

Even as he spoke, Fat Jack was ramming another charge into the swivel gun. He aimed down into the longboat and fired. Water and pieces of wood flew up into the air. The longboat shuddered and settled slowly into the shallow water. Fat Jack lifted the swivel gun from its mount and dumped it into the water. Within minutes the three men were making their way from the beach.

Above them, the same sea gull which had raised the alarm now circled unseen in the night sky. It was bigger than most of its kind and mottled with ragged spots of brown and gray. It circled high above the men for a while, then turned sharply and dove down low over the beach. It glided silently between the dunes until it picked out the lone figure who had watched the whole scene played out from behind a driftwood stump. A girl with long black hair and dressed in a homespun buckskin robe and leggins stepped from the shadows as the gull approached and landed easily on her upraised hand.

"Well done, old friend Mariah, Lord of Wind and Sea. But now I must ask you to fly once more and carry my message to the one called Jem. Make him know that he is needed here," she said as she slipped something over the gull's neck.

5

2

"No! You ain't goin', and I ain't listenin' ta no more argument 'bout it," Uncle Moss Tatum was saying crossly as he shook his finger so hard that ashes fell from his pipe. His eyebrows rose to bushy points on his forehead. "You're a mighty long way from bein' big enough ta go sailin' off with them Coast Guards a lookin' for Mexicans what are most likely smart enough to be sittin' back in Mexico a takin' their siesta."

"Aw heck," was young Jeremiah Dundee's only reply as he stepped out of the path of the drifting ashes and then shuffled his feet in the sandy street. As a final, defiant gesture, he thrust his hands so far down into the pockets of his pants that one of his suspenders came loose.

"Now Jem, my lad, just cause you're fixin' to turn thirteen don't mean you're growed up yet," Uncle Moss added in a slightly more understanding voice. Then, he turned away from the crowd gathered at McKinnie's Wharf and started walking back toward Water Street.

Jem, as everyone had called him for as long as he could remember, was a sort of nickname for Jeremiah. Jem had mixed feelings about it. Mostly, he liked it because it was so different, and he had never known anyone else with the same name. Also, it was short and easy to say, which saved a lot of unnecessary talking. On the other hand, since it was so easy to say, he sometimes wondered if that made it easier for Uncle Moss to yell at him.

"Jem!" Uncle Moss yelled at him from down the street. "Don't be standin' round a wastin' time all day now. We got sails to mend back at the loft."

Jem squinted from behind his freckled cheeks and wrinkled his nose. "I'll be along," he assured him half-heartedly and immediately turned his attention back to the activity on McKinnie's Wharf.

Once again there were rumors of war in the Republic of Texas. Talk of an invasion by Mexico was everywhere on the streets. Some believed there would be an attack by sea, while others insisted that it would be by land across the Rio Grande. The Rio Grande seemed very far away, and Jem doubted that anything happening there could possibly have an effect on his life in Galveston.

Most of the practical-minded citizens of Galveston, the ones who were dull, boring, and usually right about such things, insisted that there would be no invasion at all. They argued that, since Commodore Moore and the Texas Navy had soundly whipped the pants off the Mexican Navy at the Battle of Campeche just last year, the Mexican government was not ready to risk any further embarassments in the Republic of Texas.

Many of these same men and women also said that the Red Rovers, as the Galveston Coast Guards were called, were nothing more than a bunch of fools who would rather go sailing off to look for a fight than stay at home to do honest labor. They recalled the time two years before, when the Red Rovers had sailed up and down the coast for two weeks in search of rumored Mexican war-ships and returned without having sighted a single for-

7

eign sail. But whatever the talk in the taverns and churches might be, the citizens of Galveston had turned out this morning to give the Red Rovers a rousing send-off. And Jem had no intention of missing any of it.

He counted fifty men dressed in red flannel shirts, white pants, and black boots hurrying aboard the little schooner *Santana*. With them were all sorts of rifles and muskets and pistols and cutlasses. It was almost as good as a Fourth-of-July party or maybe San Jacinto Day.

The band was playing and women were waving scarves and handkerchiefs as the schooner cast off from the wharf and picked up a towline from one of the little steam tugs that worked in the harbor. A cheer went up as the Lone Star Flag of the Republic of Texas was hoisted to her main gaff and fluttered in the brisk northerly breeze. Jem watched until the schooner had been towed out over the bar and set her sails before he reluctantly turned for home.

Still, Jem did not feel ready to face the day's work of repairing sails at Uncle Moss's sail loft. Spring was almost here, and his thoughts drifted to adventure. It would be fun to sail his own little boat, the *Falcon,* up into Trinity Bay again and explore some of the islands and bayous he had bypassed so hurriedly last summer. But summer was still a long way off and, even then, there was no guarantee that he would have the time to do anything but work in the sail loft. Besides, he did not want to go alone.

Last summer his best friend Raif had sailed with him, but that had been different — much different. Raif was practical-minded; he just did not go off looking for adventures for no good reason.

The Tremont Hotel stood on the corner of Water Street and The Strand. Although it was almost two blocks out of his way, Jem managed to pass it on his way back to the sail loft. Raif was on the porch, but Jem was surprised to see another boy using his shoeshine box and

8

busily polishing the black boots of an English sea captain.

"Hey Jem, my friend," Raif called to him and strolled down off the porch.

Jem squinted at the boy shining shoes. "Ain't that your box?"

"Sure it is my box. I just hired that guy to work it for me."

"What?"

"I got four shoeshine boxes, so I got four other kids working for me now. José is working Shaw's Hotel, and Albert is at Alphonse's Boarding House. I got little Joey Brighton down at the Morgan Line Wharf; that's going to be good territory pretty soon. And me? I just sort of circulate wherever I am needed. And of course I collect the money and pay the help."

"That's good, I guess," Jem said with little enthusiasm as he kicked an oyster shell down the street. It skipped between the front legs of J. A. Sauter's horse, which was harnessed to his delivery wagon, and landed somewhere under the wooden sidewalk. The horse rolled its brown eyes in Jem's direction, snorted once, and looked away as if disgusted with young boys who had nothing better to do than bother sleepy horses.

"Your Uncle Moss would not let you go with the Red Rovers?" Raif asked, seeing that his friend was not happy.

"They took dumb Ralph Corbitt, and he never been on a ship in his life."

"But he's fifteen and big as a cracker barrel."

"Ain't much smarter than one neither," Jem insisted with his lower lip drooping almost to his chin.

Raif leaned against the porch railing and yawned. "That is a trip I would not worry about missing very much. They will just sail around until they run out of food and then come back empty handed just like they always do."

9

"It'd be better than just sittin' round here," Jem countered, dropping to the hotel steps.

"For me, I hope they find nothing. Wars are bad for business. People don't take time to get their shoes shined when there is a war going on."

"Think I'll go crusin' up the bay again, come summer. I still got the map and — "

Raif, who was just in the process of sitting down also, suddenly jumped to his feet. "What you want to go back up there for? Have you forgot we almost got ourselves killed last summer?"

"I ain't forgot. And I ain't forgot we found the treasure that bought your shoeshine boxes." Jem reminded him.

"Sure we found it, and we got chased by Muldoon and his apes; we saw ghosts and almost got drowned in that storm. Worst of all, I almost starved to death. Now to me, those are all real good reasons for a couple of little kids like us to stay right here and take things easy." With that, he sat down and leaned back against a banister pole.

Jem knew he was right. That was one of the dangedest things about Raif — he was practical. He and Jem were the same age, and already Raif controlled the shoeshine business in the whole city of Galveston. That was even a greater accomplishment for him than it would be for some other boys his age. Raif's father had come to Texas from Mexico before the war and had fought alongside General Sam Houston at the Battle of San Jacinto. After the war, he had become a fisherman, and one day he had sailed out into the gulf and never come back. Afterward, his mother had barely managed a meager existence doing washing and sewing.

Raif had been helping out for as long as he could remember by polishing shoes or carrying luggage for travelers at the hotels and boarding houses. Raif had a head for business. Since last summer, he had invested some of his share of the treasure to expand his shoeshine business, and now he made more money than his mother.

10

Jem was certain that his friend would be mayor before he was twenty.

"There's still a bunch of places on the map to explore," Jem added lamely.

"For what?" Raif wanted to know. "There is nothing else up there except more trouble. Look Jem, we found the treasure last summer. So let's enjoy it. What are you going to do with yours anyway?"

"Uncle Moss says that when I'm fifteen, he'll use it to pay a ship's captain to take me to sea and teach me 'bout navigatin' and sailin' and all so I can be a captain someday.

"Course, he still wants me to stay here and keep on being a sailmaker, so I can take over the business some day and he can retire."

Raif scratched his chin in deep thought. "I think there is a good future in sailmaking. Steam engines are all right, I guess. But they could never replace sails for crossing the ocean."

"I don't want to be no sailmaker all my life."

Raif shrugged, "Well then, I do not see anything wrong with being a sea captain, if you want to go sailing off all over the world and only come home every two or three years."

Jem rose slowly. "Only thing wrong is, it ain't gonna start happening for another two years. 'Till then, I'm just stuck here with nothin' to do but fix sails." He kicked at another oyster shell and started off down the street toward the sail loft.

Up until a year ago, Jem had believed he was an orphan. He had no idea where he came from or who his parents were. For as long as he could remember, he had lived in a little room above the sail loft owned by Moss Tatum and Jeffery Reid.

"Ya come here on the brig *Laura D,*" Uncle Moss (who of course was not really his uncle) had told him patiently each time he asked. "They was two days out of Campeche and runnin' 'round the west end of Scorpion Reef when the lookout spied a bit of wreckage with you on it. Not more than a babe, ya was, clingin' to a jib boom and near dead. Ya had that locket there around yer neck. They brung ya here and we took ya in. We gave ya the name Dundee 'cause the *Laura D* was named for a Lady Dundee. That's all we know, 'cause they never found out what ship it was wrecked on the reef."

Last summer everything had changed. It had started when Jem and Raif discovered an old map which was to lead them on a long and dangerous voyage far up into Galveston Bay. Before the adventure had ended, they had found a buried treasure and Jem had learned who his father was. But to Jem, knowing became a greater burden than not knowing had ever been.

His father was Jean Lafitte, a strange and mysterious figure of whom Jem still knew only bits and pieces. He had learned that his gold locket with the black falcon on it had belonged to his mother and that it was a symbol of protection, given by his father to a chosen few.

During the past year, Jem had tried to learn more about his father. Always being careful not to show too much interest, he had asked a few old-timers who claimed to have met Lafitte at one time or another. Most remembered him as a pirate chieftain who once built a fortress called Maison Rouge on what was now the outskirts of the city. They said that the United States Navy had accused him of attacking American ships and that he had set fire to his fortress and then sailed away to the Yucatan. Most scoffed at rumors that he was still alive and insisted that he had been killed in a duel with the English officer and was buried somewhere along the Yucatan Coast.

Jem knew different. Now he carried the secret, known only to himself, Raif, and two other trusted friends who were now far away.

At the front door of the sail loft, Jem stopped long enough to watch his own little sailboat, the *Falcon,* as she bobbed at her mooring alongside the pier. She seemed to be restless as she tugged against the north wind, dipping her bow to each of the white-capped waves which marched across the anchorage. He thought nothing of the large gray and brown sea gull which was perched on top of the mast.

Stepping inside the loft, he found Uncle Moss with a pair of scissors in his hand cutting away on a huge piece of heavy canvas spread out on the floor. From its shape, Jem knew it was going to be a yankee jib for the English Barkentine that was loading cotton at the wharfs. Jeffery Reid was at his desk near the door adding and subtracting long lines of figures in a ledger book. Neither man paid Jem much notice as he gathered up his sailor's palm, needles, and waxed thread and went to work.

It was after ten o'clock that night before Jem slipped off to his room above the loft. He opened his one window to the night sky and lit his coal oil lamp. From beneath his cot, he carefully removed the old treasure map, his father's map, which he and Raif had followed last summer.

In the flickering lamplight, he traced the faded lines with his finger as he had done countless times before. There were so many places he had not visited. There was the river called San Jacinto, which the steamboats used to go to Harrisburg and Houston. To the northeast of it were many bayous which ran together, and among them was a symbol which looked something like a cannon. To the east was Trinity Bay and above it the Trinity River, which wound its way north. On the upper edge was an arrow and a note which read "Camp de Isle." Jem had no idea what it meant, but he was afraid to show the map to anyone who might know.

The settlement of Anahuac was marked where the Trinity River emptied into Trinity Bay. South of it were several bayous, some with names and some without. There were also many small islands, but only one had a name. It was called "Vingt-et-un," and Jem also wondered what that meant.

There was a sudden rustle of cool wind through the window. The lamp flame flickered, sending strange shadows dancing across the wall. Jem looked up, startled as a cold chill went up his spine. For a moment the shadow seemed to be a serpent, then a bird, and then nothing but meaningless shapes.

Rising from his cot, Jem started to close the window and almost bumped into the big sea gull which now stood just inside. He backed up a few steps, tripped against the cot, and found himself sitting down again.

The bird eyed him with a slightly cocked head but did not move. Likewise, it did not move when Jem finally found his voice and waved his rolled-up map. "Get outa here, ya silly old bird," he ordered in an uncertain voice. This was the biggest sea gull Jem had ever seen, and it showed no fear of him whatsoever. For several long minutes bird and boy stared at each other before the lamplight reflected off of something shiny around the bird's neck.

Slowly, Jem's curiosity overcame his fear and he moved cautiously toward the silent bird. Other than for an occasional cocking of its head, the bird stood motionless as Jem approached. Around its neck and half hidden among gray and brown feathers was a leather string. Jem's first thought was that the bird had become tangled in something and wanted Jem to remove it. "Now be a nice bird and don't go bittin' me or nothin'," he said quietly as he reached for the string. The bird made no protest as Jem's fingers touched the string, carefully slipped it over the bird's head, and passed its large curved beak. Only then did he see the golden ornament which was attached to it.

"Talva?" he whispered.

3

Under the flickering lantern light, Jem examined the cross as a strange chill went up his spine. It was gold but with a greenish cast. Above the crucifix was a skull and crossbones. Below it was a scroll with a few letters whose meaning he did not know.

"It's gotta be hers," he whispered to himself. "I ain't never seen another one like it."

He thought of the night they had divided the treasure, that last night when Raif, Talva, Crazy Ben, and himself had been together. Their campfire burned low on the bluff near Morgan's Point, and in the distance, the little *Falcon* was bobbing at anchor. There were three neat piles of coins because Ben had, for his own reasons, refused to take a share.

Only two items were left undivided, and Jem had had little interest in either one. There was a golden necklace which Raif asked to keep as a present for his mother, and there was the cross. Talva had turned it in her hands several times and said, "This has been many places and seen many things, few of them pleasant. It would bring you no luck, but for me, it could be useful."

"Take it," Raif had agreed with no second thoughts. "I do not want anything to do with some spooky old cross."

Jem had nodded his agreement. Talva threaded the cross on a leather thong and hung it around her neck. The division had been complete.

"Now what's it doin' on some ol bird?" Jem wondered aloud. He looked up at the open window. The sea gull had vanished, and the curtains were rustling in the wind.

"I gotta tell Raif," Jem decided after a long moment. Tucking the cross into his pocket, he hid his map under the mattress and climbed out the window. A narrow ledge led to the corner of the building, and from there it was an easy jump to the roof of the warehouse next door. In less than a minute he had slid down the gutter pipe and was on the street.

Raif's house was about ten minutes away, but tonight Jem made the trip in half that time by cutting across a couple of back yards. Unfortunately, he woke up old Mrs. Gruber's goat who butted him in the pants just once before he got over the fence and into the next yard where he was chased by Paul Jacob's big shaggy dog. By the time he reached the outskirts of Galveston, there was a considerable amount of barking and braying behind him and several lamps had been lit along his path.

Raif lived with his mother in a little house set off by itself on a low hill surrounded by a few salt cedars. It was an old house, built of rough timbers, but now it was neatly painted and there was even a small flower bed near the front door. Jem remembered that a year ago it had been a rundown shack. Some of Raif's treasure had gone to fix up the old house, buy his mother a new cook stove, and even put real glass in the downstairs windows.

Jem tossed an oyster shell at the loft window and waited. There was no answer, so he tossed another and then another before Raif's head finally appeared. "Go away," he grumbled. "It's the middle of the night and I just got to sleep."

Jem whispered as loud as he could. "Come outside; it's real important!"

Raif shook his head. "What is real important is that this little kid gets some sleep tonight. I will see you tomorrow."

Again Jem shook his head. "It's about Talva! She's in some sort of trouble."

Raif stared down at him, then nodded his head and disappeared back inside. Jem was not sure if he was coming down or if he had just gone back to sleep. He was looking for another oyster shell to throw when Raif at last came out the front door. He staggered immediately to one of the cedar trees, sat down with his back against the trunk, and closed his eyes. "Okay, I am here, but talk fast, this kid is sleepy."

Jem excitedly told him about the sea gull and the cross. When he had finished, Raif only yawned and said, "Tomorrow I am going to tell you about this silly dream I had. In this dream you came to my house in the middle of the night and were babbling about this big bird that flew in your window and gave you Talva's cross."

"It ain't no dream, dang it! That's what happened."

Raif sighed heavily and opened one eye. "Maybe Talva lost the cross and this sea gull just picked it up. They like shiny things sometimes."

"So why'd he bring it to me then?"

"I do not know. But, whatever the reason is, we can talk about it tomorrow."

"Can't wait 'till then. We gotta go right now!" Jem insisted.

"Not so loud," Raif warned him, pointing at the house. "You are going to wake up my mother." Raif got to his feet and continued. "Go? Where do you think you are going to go? You don't have any idea where to find Talva."

Jem hesitated, realizing that he had not given that

much thought. "Back up where we met her last time, I reckon."

"You know how Talva is, she just wanders all over the place doing whatever she wants. She could be anywhere now."

"She sent us a message; she wants us to come and find her!"

"This is your message, not mine. Besides, we just can't go off for no reason."

"We got a reason now."

"You got a cross that you think is the one we gave to Talva. That does not sound like much of a message."

"Does ta me."

Raif yawned and started for the house. "Then you go find her and tell her hello for me. I am going back to bed."

"I'm sailin' in the mornin'," Jem said.

Raif stopped in his tracks. "You are crazy. What do you want to find that spooky old girl for anyway?"

Jem scuffed his feet in the sand and did not answer as Raif started walking back toward him. "Is there something else you are not telling me?"

"I just got a feelin', that's all."

"I don't want to hear anything about your feelings; they always get me in trouble."

"All right then, I ain't gonna tell ya nothin' else. But, we gotta leave in the mornin."

"We!" Raif almost yelled in his face. "Who is this 'we' you are talking about? I myself, Rafael Don Marcos Rodrigues Fernando Garcia, am going nowhere with you in a boat ever again. Everyday I thank the Virgin Mary that I survived my first, last, and only adventure. Now the only place I am going is back to bed and in the morning I have to get up and go work."

Jem watched as he started for the house. "That mean you ain't goin' with me?"

Raif stopped once again and turned slowly back to face him. "Yes, my friend, that means I am not going

18

with you and I hope you come to your senses before morning and don't go either.

"I gotta go. Ain't nothin' gonna change it."

Raif shook his head and turned away. "Then be careful and do not get yourself drowned or something."

Jem watched him disappear into the house and stood staring at the closed door for a while hoping in vain that Raif might suddenly change his mind and return.

He did not.

At last Jem started back toward town. He had to admit that this was a crazy idea. How could he expect anyone to take him seriously? "Maybe I am crazy," he said to himself as he walked. But the old feeling was returning. That feeling of being 'pulled' toward some place far away. He had felt it before when he and Raif used to visit the ruins of the pirate fort called Maison Rouge. Raif had never understood, but Jem had known even then that somehow his destiny was tied to it. Now he was feeling it again, stronger than ever, urging him to go, to set the sails on *Falcon* and be off. Perhaps he was meant to go alone this time. It was his destiny, not Raif's, that he was seeking. Still, it would be lonely without him. It would also be hard to sail the *Falcon* all by himself. But there seemed to be no choice, and grimly, he accepted the challenge.

The rest of the night he spent gathering a few needed items. From Uncle Moss's pantry he took a loaf of bread, a small bag of black beans, some salt beef, and dried fruit. He filled two bottles with water from the well and took some extra coal oil for his lantern. His fishing line, extra rope, and a small cast net were already aboard his boat where he always kept them.

A light fog had settled over Galveston when Jem finally decided that it was almost daybreak and he could spend no more time getting ready. He would have to sail with what he had. Rolling everything into a blanket, he took his map and headed for the docks.

The *Falcon* was waiting for him, still tugging nervously at her moorings. Jem kept an old piece of sail tied like a tent over the boom to keep out rainwater. Beneath it was a bag containing the *Falcon's* sails and some spare lines. Jem decided to rearrange it all to make room for the rest of his stuff. In the darkness, he stepped aboard and reached in under the tarp expecting to touch damp canvas. Instead, his hand found something warm and soft. There was the rustle of movement from beneath the sailbag, and the *Falcon* rolled slightly. A hand grabbed his arm almost before Jem realized that someone had been hiding on the boat.

4

Jerking his hand away, Jem fell backward against the *Falcon's* tiller and almost went overboard. One of the ropes holding the tarp broke under his weight and collapsed into a wiggling mass. Jem grabbed the first thing his hand touched, which happened to be an oar. Whatever manner of creature was beneath his tarp, it began to rise slowly into a ghostly, shapeless phantom, still drapped beneath the tarp. Jem raised the oar above his head and was ready to strike when a sleepy voice said. "Is it time to get up already?"

"Raif?" Jem asked, lowering the oar.

"Of course, it's me. Who else would be out here this time of the morning?" came the voice from beneath the tarp. At last, Raif's head appeared.

"What in tarnation you doin' here?"

Raif yawned and sat down against *Falcon's* mast. "Oh, I just thought I would try one more time to talk you out of this crazy trip you are going to take."

"Well, it ain't gonna do no good," Jem insisted hotly. "I gotta go and that's all there is to it."

Raif nodded his head slowly, and Jem was surprised that he did not seem to want to argue with him anymore. "Yes, I figured that would be the case. You are so bull-headed that there is never any chance of talking sense to you." He stood up then and began loading Jem's scattered gear into the boat. When Jem just stared at him, Raif said, "Well, come on, let's get going; you said you wanted to be sailing by sunrise."

"You goin' with me?" Jem asked stupidly.

Raif continued to load gear. "Of course I am going with you. That does not mean I think it is a good idea, and I am sure my shoeshine business will fall apart while I am gone. But I am going for the same reason I always go with you. We are friends, partners. And besides, some-body has got to keep you out of trouble."

Jem rose and tried to say thanks but Raif cut him off. "Do not thank me. Let's just get going because I know that, before very long, I am going to be sorry I did this."

In silence then, they stowed their gear and hoisted the *Falcon's* sails. Jem took the tiller as Raif cast off the mooring lines, and they headed out into the harbor. The first rays of sunshine peeked over the horizon and painted the eastern sky a dozen shades of soft pink.

Most of Jem's free time during the past year had been spent improving the *Falcon's* sail plan. Little by lit-tle he had changed her old "leg-o-mutton" rig which con-sisted of only one loose-footed sail. He added a boom he had built from the flagstaff of a wrecked brig. A jib sail was cut from scraps of canvas left in the sail loft. He had even added a two-foot bowsprit which now stuck out ahead of *Falcon's* bow at an angle designed for speed. But his long hours of work had paid off. *Falcon* now sailed as close to the wind as any craft in Galveston Bay, and even the harbor pilot's schooner had a hard time keeping up with her in light air.

The ruins of Maison Rouge stood gaunt and dark against the dawn sky as they sailed past the lonely hill just east of town. As they rounded Pelican Island, they

23

found a stiff north wind driving a steady line of white-caps across the bay. The *Falcon* heeled sharply and dipped her rail. Spray blew across her bow as Jem tightened his grip on the tiller, and they bounded off toward the northeast.

Raif pulled the old tarp around his shoulders to keep off some of the spray and asked, "Where are we bound for?"

"Wind's from the north, so I reckon if we keep sailin' this direction, we ought to find the islands we got wrecked on last summer."

Raif nodded and was silent for a long time. There was only the whine of wind in the rigging and the gurgling of water hurrying past the *Falcon's* hull. "You think you will find your father this time, don't you?" he asked at length.

Jem looked away, avoiding his eyes, and shrugged.

"That's what your 'feeling' is really all about, isn't it?"

"Maybe; maybe not," Jem answered, still avoiding Raif's eyes. "And maybe I'll never know nothin' about my father 'cept what he wrote in that letter he left me in the treasure chest."

Jem had read that letter only twice before he burned it, but every word would remain forever engraved in his mind. It had said that the treasure was his and that he had proved himself worthy by finding it. His father had written that the world thought he was dead and that was best for now. He had ended with the lines: "Farewell my son. Perhaps some day we will meet, perhaps not." It was signed, "Your father, Jean Lafitte."

The *Falcon* beat her way into the north wind all morning. It was an uncomfortable passage, and by noon everything aboard was wet from flying spray. The islands of Red Fish Bar were still barely visible ahead. Raif bailed water and stayed huddled under the tarp while Jem steered.

"You think we will reach the islands before dark?" Raif asked as he peeked his head out from under the tarp long enough to look ahead.

24

"Hope so," Jem answered, trying to sound confident, "The wind's against us and the tide is running out, too. It might be pretty late."

The afternoon passed with the wind staying out of the north. The sun was quite low by the time the islands were still a mile ahead. Raif was sitting with the tarp pulled over his head looking toward the land. He was cold, wet, hungry, and already beginning to have second thoughts about coming along on this trip.

"I do not see how we are going to find anyone up here unless maybe you'll have another dream about a big sea gull that brings us messages," he said sarcastically and flapped his arms like wings underneath the tarp.

"That weren't no danged dream," Jem insisted just as the big sea gull swooped down and landed squarely on Raif's head.

Raif said nothing but froze with his arms still extended. His eyes got big and rolled upward. "Jem," he said in almost a whisper, "please tell me that this thing on my head is not what I think it is."

Jem was laughing too hard to answer him.

"Go on now, bird, get away from me," Raif wailed, and the bird took flight only long enough to move to the bowsprit where it settled itself once again. Neither boy was sure where it had come from, but Jem assumed that it had been circling above them with its back to the sun before it had suddenly swooped down to land on Raif's head.

Jem said, "It's the same bird, I'm sure of it."

"That is a pretty big gull," Raif commented, still embarrassed at being frightened by anything so common.

"Ain't that just what I told you?"

Raif ignored his question and asked, "Does he have a name?"

"How would I know? It ain't like I been talkin' to him."

Raif held out the remains of a tortilla he had been eating. "Maybe he is hungry?" he suggested, but the gull ignored his offering and flew off into the air. He circled

25

the boat once and then turned away to the southeast. In a few minutes he was back again, sitting on the *Falcon's* bowsprit. As evening drew nearer, the bird would alternately sit on the bowsprit and fly off, always in the same direction only to return a short time later.

"You reckon he wants us to follow him?" Jem asked.

Raif shrugged his shoulders. "I don't know. What is there over that way?"

Jem pulled his map out of his shirt and together they looked at it. "I figure we're somewhere along in here," he said, putting his finger on a spot just south of some of the islands of Red Fish Bar. To the northeast was a point of land called Smith Point. Due east was a line of tiny dots named Hanna's Reef. Several miles southeast was Bolivar Island, a long narrow peninsula of land which separated Galveston Bay from the Gulf of Mexico.

"Ain't much of anything out there, least ways that shows on this map."

"Then I think we should sail to the nearest land, build a fire, get warm, and cook supper," Raif advised.

Jem had the strange feeling that he should follow the sea gull, but he was also cold and wet and hungry. The islands to the north did not look very far away and it was almost dark now, so he agreed with Raif and held his course.

The wind dropped off some as darkness closed in around them. There was no moon. A few scattered clouds hid many of the stars as the *Falcon* sailed slowly along. Jem noticed that he could barely see the bow.

"Keep a good watch up forward," he told Raif, "and listen for the sound of waves breaking, so we'll know when we were getting close to land."

The hours slipped quietly by, but when the moon finally rose, the *Falcon* was within a few hundred yards of a small island with several cedar trees clinging to its center. Jem steered into the island's lea and beached the *Falcon* on a white shell beach which seemed to glow in the moonlight.

26

Together, they furled the sail and tied the anchor line to a driftwood log. In the shelter of the cedars, Raif soon had a campfire crackling and a pot of beans and salt pork simmering over it.

"Do you think we are far from where we met Talva last summer?" Raif asked after they had eaten.

"I don't think it's very far," Jem yawned. "But if we don't find her by tomorrow night, I think we should sail south, the way the sea gull flew."

"I remember once she told us that her mother had lived on Lone Oak Bayou. Maybe we should go there?"

Jem picked up his blanket and moved closer to the fire. "Yeah, maybe," he yawned, "but I'm too tired to figure our next move now."

The moon was high. Scattered clouds raced across the southern sky as the boys rolled up in their blankets. The north wind sang in the twisted cedars above them, the campfire burned low, and the distant lapping of waves on the beach lulled them into a peaceful, dreamless sleep.

They did not see the big sea gull that flew in from the south and circled the island once before coming to roost on the top of the *Falcon's* mast.

5

Jem awoke with the big sea gull sitting on his chest. "Get away, ya old bird," he grumbled and burrowed deeper into his blanket. The sea gull flapped its wings, then walked around and pecked him on the head.

"Ouch," Jem yelled and grabbed at the bird, which easily moved just out of his reach. He sat up, rubbed his head, and looked around, "Well, I reckon you're gonna be with us awhile yet."

The north wind was blowing a gray morning mist in swirls around the island. Their campfire was only ashes, and everything was damp from mist and dew. But the salt air felt fresh and clean. There was a hint of sunshine in the east. Other gulls were circling and diving over the water. A few shore birds ran up and down the beach, fishing in the shallows.

Raif was still snoring, so Jem walked down to the beach. He eventually walked all the way around the island. At one point he found the ashes of another campfire. It was a large one, not the kind Talva would have made. It was built against a driftwood log, and he wondered if it had been done to make it hard to see from the bay.

A point of land was visible to the east, only about a half mile away, and several other islands stretched out to the west. They were all small, and only a few had trees. He saw nothing familiar about any of them.

By the time he returned to camp, Raif was awake. He had the fire burning and was brewing tea from a little, cheesecloth bag he had brought along. The sea gull was standing nearby, polishing its beak on an oyster shell.

"That bird pecked me," Raif accused, pointing his finger.

"You too, huh?"

"He is spooky. He just stands around waiting for us to get going."

"I think he wants us to hurry up," Jem said as he began gathering up their gear.

They sailed north that morning and reached the island where they had been wrecked and met Talva last summer. They spent an hour combing it but found nothing to indicate that anyone had been there for a long time.

"Well," Jem sighed, pointing at the big sea gull who was once again sitting on the *Falcon's* mast, "I reckon we follow the bird now."

So all that afternoon they retraced their course south. The north wind was dropping off, and it was early evening when they passed between the mainland and the island they had camped on the night before. The sea gull flew off to the southeast, and Jem turned the *Falcon* to follow him.

When darkness overtook them, the land was far behind. Only open water lay ahead.

Raif took the tiller and Jem crawled up under the tarp to get some sleep. "Reckon we'll be sailin' all night, so we'll stand watches. Wake me up when you get sleepy."

The *Falcon* sailed slowly south in the darkness for several hours. They had no compass, and clouds were covering most of the stars, so Raif steered by keeping the wind over his left shoulder. He stared into the darkness for hours and listened for the sound of waves breaking, which would mean they were close to shore. The first sounds he heard were human voices.

"Jem!" Raif called as he poked at him. "I hear people out there — somewhere close!"

Jem came awake with a start and sat up. "Where are they an' what are they saying?" he asked sleepily.

"I can't make it out, but there is something over there," Raif answered, pointing to the east. Jem could just see a dark shadow which looked like a boat. It carried a leg-o-mutton sail similar to the rig the *Falcon* had originally carried, but it was at least twice as big and sailing toward them.

"Longboat or a lugger," Jem said. "Wander what it's doin' out here?" Even as he spoke, two more shadows appeared ahead of the *Falcon*. "Look, there's two more behind it."

Raif touched his arm and pointed the other direction. "And there's another one. *Madre Maria,* there is a whole fleet of them!"

Very close along the *Falcon's* starboard side, they could see yet a fifth longboat, also moving on the same course. A voice called out in the night and was answered by others from the other boats.

"What'd they say?" Jem asked.

"They are speaking Spanish," Raif answered. "They are trying to find a pass over Red Fish Bar."

"You reckon they're fishermen?" Jem whispered.

"I do not think so. One man is giving all the orders and the others are calling him 'lieutenant.' It sounds like they are off of some ship, but I do not understand why they would be out here."

"Maybe they're pirates," Jem whispered.

"I don't know who they are, but I think we should get

out of here just as fast as we can." But even as Raif spoke, Jem was turning the *Falcon* to sail the same direction as the other boats.

Raif whispered loudly in Jem's ear, "What are you doing? We want to go the other way — *any* way except along with them.

"We can't. They'd spot us for sure if we turned away. But it's pretty dark. Maybe if we sail with them, they'll figure we're one of their boats. If we turn away now, they'll know something is wrong."

"But they will see us!" Raif wailed, unable to sit still.

"Maybe not before we can find the right time to turn away."

A few tense moments passed and a Spanish voice called out of the night. "He's talking to us!" Raif almost cried. "He wants to know if we can still see the other boats."

"Well then, answer him in Spanish."

With great concentration Raif calmed himself, took a deep breath, and spoke in his deepest voice. Then he let out a great sigh of relief and whispered, "I told him we can see all of them."

You think he believed you?"

"For a little while, maybe. Maybe we might even get away with this until the moon comes up, but then they will see us for sure and we are going to be in all kinds of trouble. I think this is a fine mess we got ourselves into."

"Reckon we shouldn't have followed that ol' sea gull after all," Jem sighed and steered to keep as much distance as possible between them and the strange boats.

Jem waited for his chance to turn the *Falcon* away and disappear into the night, but the chance did not come. The strange boats continued north and kept getting closer and closer together. Twice more the *Falcon* was hailed, and Raif used his deep voice to assure them that everything was all right.

A voice called across the water and was answered by another out of the darkness. Raif whistled quietly be-

32

tween his teeth and then whispered excitedly. "Jem, you know what they were just talking about?"

"Course I don't know what they're talkin' about. I don't speak Spanish."

"One of those men asked someone in another boat if that little girl had bitten him again! And then the other one told him he didn't see why they were keeping her, and they ought to throw her to the sharks!"

The two boys stared at each other and then both whispered at the same moment, "Talva?"

6

"We gotta rescue her," Jem whispered.

"How we going to do that? It seems to me that we have all we can do just keeping ourselves from getting caught."

"I don't know, but we gotta think of somethin' fast. The moon is fixin' ta rise and when it does, they'll see us for sure." The eastern horizon was already glowing pale yellow. In a very few minutes, the bay would be in moonlight and then there would be little chance that *Falcon* could continue to masquerade as one of the longboats.

"Which boat is she on?" he asked Raif.

I think that one."

"Okay, let's go," Jem ordered as he hauled in the *Falcon's* sail and turned her closer to the wind.

"Let's go?" Raif's disturbed voice came through the night. "Let's go where? What are we going to do?"

"I got a plan, sort of. We'll sail up from behind them and I'll try to hit their rudder. You take the oar and hit the first one you can reach and — "

"You call that a plan?" Raif whispered. "That's nothing but a plan to get us in more trouble!"

The *Falcon* was gathering speed on her new course just as the moon touched the horizon. The shapes of the surrounding boats became clear in pale light as the *Falcon* quickly closed the distance between themselves and the longboat they believed Talva was aboard. Jem aimed his bow at the longboat's rudder and hauled in his mainsail another few inches. At the bow, he could see Raif standing with a raised oar.

Suddenly, the dark figure of a man at the longboat's tiller turned and looked directly at them. *"Buenos Noches,"* Raif said and swung his oar.

The man staggered under the blow just as the *Falcon* collided with the longboat's rudder. The *Falcon's* mast shuddered from the impact, but the longboat's tiller swung hard over. There was the sound of cracking wood as it caught the man in the stomach and knocked him down into the boat.

"Talva, come on! Jump for it!" Raif was yelling as they scraped past the longboat's stern, and Jem could see its rudder hanging, broken at an odd angle. He grabbed at it and tried to turn the *Falcon* alongside. There were at least four other men and a large pile of heavy wooden crates in the longboat. For one fleeting moment they saw Talva. Her hands were tied, and one of the men was holding her. The other two were trying to grab the *Falcon's* rail.

It was too late. Jem knew the rescue had failed. Now they would be lucky to escape themselves. Hopelessly, he turned the *Falcon* away.

"No, Jem! I can't reach her. We have to go back," Raif was shouting as he swung the oar wildly at anything that moved.

"I can't; we gotta run for it!" Jem yelled. He laid the *Falcon* on her fastest point of sail and, with the wind abeam, trimmed his sails.

He gave no thought to which direction he was

headed and did not care. All around them the strange fleet of longboats was in confusion, but one fact was certain: they were all chasing the *Falcon*. The night was filled with shouting and cursing as two of the boats rammed together and someone fell overboard. Another boat crossed their bow and Jem edged the *Falcon* closer to the wind to slip by. He could see men desperately backing their oars and trying to stop the forward movement of their boat, but it was to late. The *Falcon* cut astern of them and was gone into the night with her rail under and white water boiling around her bow.

A pistol shot rang out, followed by another, and then another. To Jem, it seemed that the whole world was shooting at them. Raif was on the floor grates with his hands over his head, and Jem sat down as low as he could and still see ahead. Musket balls whined around them, putting neat little holes in the *Falcon's* sail and sending splinters flying from her rail.

"I told you I was going to be sorry I came with you!" Raif moaned.

Jem looked desperately around for some route of escape. The moon had nearly cleared the horizon now, and he could plainly see four boats in hot pursuit. The moonlight also revealed a bank of clouds off the *Falcon's* bow. As Jem watched, lightning flashed from somewhere behind them. He swallowed hard and steered for the storm. "Reckon we'll be hard enough to find in there," he announced solemnly.

The *Falcon* raced on. Soon she was outdistancing her heavily loaded pursuers. Fifteen minutes later, the first raindrops began to fall and then a strong gust of wind slammed into them, rolling the *Falcon* almost on her side before Jem freed the jib sheet and regained control. With her jib streaming out over the bow, the *Falcon* flew before the storm like the bird for which she was named. Jem and Raif could do little but hold on as the rain drove down on them in cold sheets, lightning flashed around them, and thunder boomed like the firing of a hundred cannon.

They lost track of time before the rain slacked and the wind dropped a little. Jem watched the line of big waves rolling up under the *Falcon's* stern and, at just the right moment, turned her into the wind. They quickly dropped the sails.

Exhausted, soaked to the skin, cold, and disappointed, they sat drifting in the rain. They rigged the tarp over the boom for protection and huddled silently beneath it as they waited for morning.

When dawn finally came, the rain had passed. Only a few clouds were left in the sky. Land was still visible to the north, but it was a long way off. Jem and Raif were both shivering so hard they could barely talk.

Raif's first words were, "We have to go back for her."

Jem nodded. "I know. I just wish I had some plan for rescuing her. Heck, I don't even know how we can find them again."

Raif looked up at the sky. "Now where's that sea gull when you need him?"

No sea gull could be seen, so they tiredly folded up the tarp, hoisted the *Falcon's* sails, and set a course for land. The wind was light and backing to the east, a sure sign of fair weather. An hour later they had spotted a line of low sand bars running north and south. None of them were big enough to have any grass or trees, and waves were breaking over some of them.

Jem took out his map and together they studied it for a while. "I reckon this might be Hanna Reef. You hear anything last night that might give us a clue to where those pirates, or whatever they are, were headed?"

Raif scratched his head. "They were looking for a pass across Red Fish Bar."

"Then they must be headed for someplace north."

And they were worried about finding it before sunrise. I think maybe they are hiding somewhere during the day and moving only at night.

37

"Then they might stop at one of them islands near where we camped." Jem was remembering the old campfire he had found the morning before when he suddenly heard a dog bark. Both boys looked around, and at first, saw nothing.

"Look there!" Raif said, pointing to a little sand bar far down the reef.

Jem squinted his eyes and could see something about the size of a big dog running back and forth on the sand bar and barking wildly.

"You know," Raif said thoughtfully. "If I did not know better, I would say that sounded like Talva's Dog, Getana."

In a moment, they had the oars out and were rowing furiously in the dog's direction. When the *Falcon* bumped the sandy bottom, they stopped and called the animal by name. The dog suddenly stopped running, cocked its head, and studied them for a moment. Then it whined and bounded into the water.

"That's Getana all right," Raif said as the shaggy yellow animal came splashing up to the *Falcon's* side. It took both of them to pull her aboard, and they almost capsized before the big, water-soaked dog had settled down.

"Hey, she remembers us!" Jem said as Getana licked his face and pushed him down against the stern.

"I bet she is thirsty." Raif poured some of their water into the bailing bucket. Getana whined her thanks and lapped the bucket dry. "I wonder how she got out here on this reef?"

"Those men who have Talva must have left her here. Reckon she would have died of thirst if we hadn't come along."

"Maybe she can help us find Talva."

"Yeah, she might help us rescue her, too. I remember she was pretty good in a fight."

Raif was feeding Getana a tortilla when he asked, "do you have another plan?"

38

"Nope," Jem answered honestly. "I ain't got any idea how we can find her again. But if we sailed back to Galveston for help, it would take too long and nobody'd believe us anyhow."

Raif frowned grimly at the far horizon. "So, my friends, we seem to have no choice but to go on."

With the easterly wind on their starboard beam, they worked the *Falcon* north to the mainland, east of the place called Smith Point and then turned west, sailing as close to shore as possible to make themselves harder to see. Thick forests grew clear to the water here, and they found no sign of boats or people.

Around noon they beached the *Falcon* behind some tall trees on Smith Point and walked across the narrow stretch of land to where they could see the islands of Red Fish Bar stretching off into the distance. Getana came ashore excitedly and ran in circles for a while, trying to pick up Talva's scent; then she followed the boys across the point and stood barking out at the distant islands.

"You think she's out there somewhere, don't you, girl?" Raif said, petting the dog's head.

Jem turned away from the beach and sat down with his head in his hands. "I can't figure no danged way we're ever gonna rescue her. If you're right and they're only travelin' at night, then they're camped out there on one of those islands and they'd see us coming a mile away if we went out there now. But if we wait until after dark, they'll be long gone before we could find 'em."

"Yes, and if I am wrong, then they are already north of the bar and far away," Raif added dejectedly and sat down next to Jem. Getana lay beside them and kept staring out toward the bay.

"What do ya figure they're carryin' in those boats?"

Raif shrugged. "I do not know, but it is in big boxes and is pretty heavy."

"It's heavy fur sure; them boats were sitting real low in the water."

"Let me see your map," Raif said with a faint glimmer of hope in his voice. Jem handed it to him, and Raif spent a long time looking at it.

"What ya thinkin'?" Jem asked, becoming impatient after several minutes.

Raif shook his head. "If these men were traveling to the other side of the bay, to Clear Creek or up to Harrisburg perhaps, do you think they would have crossed the bar this far east? It seems like it would be easier to cross by Red Fish Island like the steamboats do."

"Yeah, so what?"

"So I figure they are headed for someplace on this side of the bay. Now, if we can figure out someplace they will have to pass along the way, then maybe we can get ahead of them and be waiting when they get there."

Jem did not answer but turned his attention to the map. North of Smith Point were only a few islands. Only the one called "Vingt-et-un" was named. It showed as a small island with a lagoon in its center. A tiny, faded anchor symbol showed along its northern shore. "Maybe here," Jem said.

"Yes, that might be a good place. Even if they only pass by, there would be a good chance we could see them if we kept a watch all night."

Jem got to his feet and rolled up the map. "I think we can reach it before dark if we hurry and if the wind holds."

The evening sun cast long shadows across the island of Vingt-et-un. Although it was not large, there was a heavy growth of trees all along its northern shore and only a small stretch of shell beach on the western end. On the south side were clumps of salt grass and cactus. A flock of red and white spoonbills rose into the sky, and sandpipers ran along the water's edge as the *Falcon* approached.

According to Jem's map, all the water near the island was only two or three feet deep except for a narrow channel which approached from the north and ended at the anchor symbol. He had doubted that this could be correct, but now, as he eased the *Falcon* in ever closer to the trees along the bank, it became clear that the map was accurate. In fact, the *Falcon* touched her bow against one of the trees with almost four feet of water still under her little keel.

Just beyond lay a tiny, hidden cove which was totally invisible from the outside world. Two trees hung out

41

over the water to cover the entrance. Behind them, and beneath a lacy network of branches, was just enough space to hide a small boat. They carefully eased the *Falcon* into the secret anchorage and rested her bow against a shell bank.

"This place is spooky," Raif announced in a whisper as Getana bounded off the boat and into the woods. "Do you think anyone knows about this?"

"My father must have known about it. He marked it on the map, just like he figured we might need it someday," Jem answered as he tied the *Falcon's* anchor line around a tree. He had almost finished before he noticed that another line was already tied to the same tree. He touched it and it broke in his hand. "Hey Raif," he called, "look at this."

As Raif approached, Jem began to trace out the old rope. It ran, mostly buried in the shell, to the edge of the water and disappeared beneath the *Falcon's* bow. He pulled on it and found that it was attached to an ancient, rotten piece of wood.

"What is it?" Raif wanted to know.

The two boys examined the relic closely. The rope was shackled to a brass ring bolted through the wood. "Looks like the stem head off a boat not much bigger than the *Falcon*."

"What's a stem head?"

"The main timber in a boat's bow," Jem told him and pointed to the *Falcon's* bow where a similar ring secured her anchor line. "So that means somebody left a boat here a long time ago and never came back for it."

"My father, maybe," Jem suggested.

"Yes, maybe," Raif agreed and then stared seriously at him for a moment. "Jem, my friend, there is something that you have to think about."

"What's that?" Jem answered, not really listening as he began to unpack some gear.

"You said you felt like your father might still be somewhere around here."

43

"Yeah, but it's just a feeling."

"But if you are right, is it not possible that these men who have Talva might by your father's crew?"

Jem stared at him and said nothing, but there was anger growing in his eyes.

"Just think about it," Raif continued uneasily. "They are traveling only at night, carrying a cargo which they are going to a lot of trouble to keep secret. And, even though they sound like they are off of some foreign ship, thoy know the aiea, they know the passes through the bar and what islands they can hide on during the day. You said yourself they might be pirates and — "

"Ben said my father weren't no pirate!" Jem cut in. "He said my father abandoned Galveston and burned his fort rather than fight Americans or Texans."

Raif nodded patiently. "Yes, I know, and I hope you are right, but I just think we should consider it."

"Ain't nothin' to consider," Jem finished the conversation and stalked off.

When twilight came, they had hidden the *Falcon* beneath a camouflage of branches. They built a small cooking fire away from the beach and behind a fallen log. They extinguished it as soon as supper was cooked.

Just before dark, the big sea gull flew in low over the water and landed on the beach beside them. Jem frowned at him, "You got us in a heap of trouble last night, ya silly ol' bird."

"Yeah," Raif agreed, "we followed you into a whole bunch of real bad men who shot at us. But, you also led us to Talva."

"Yeah," Jem admitted grudgingly. "Wish he could of given us a little warning first."

Raif nodded. "True, my friend. But I think that is what he is doing now."

"Huh?"

"I mean, we have not seen him since yesterday morning. I think he is telling us that we are in the right place to see them again tonight."

44

" 'Fraid ya might be right," Jem admitted.

Beneath a cluster of cedar trees on the island's highest point, they settled down to watch as darkness closed in around them. Raif took the first watch. About ten o'clock, he woke Jem and lay down with his head against a tree. He was quickly sound asleep.

Jem sat alone, looking out across the wide expanse of Galveston Bay. The constellation which Talva had called "The Drinking Gourd," but sailors knew as the Big Dipper, seemed to be pouring water on Texas. Orion, the hunter, was high in the western sky, followed by his faithful Dog Star, Sirius.

Could Raif be right? he wondered. Could these men who were holding Talva be his father's? If they were, then they would know of the secret anchorage, and they would approach from the north, just as he had. And if they did, they would find the *Falcon* and know immediately he was on the island. Then there would be no escape.

He forced the unpleasant thoughts out of his mind and stood up. The moon would be rising soon and then he would be able to see much farther out onto the bay. Raif was sound asleep.

One thing about Raif, he thought, no matter how much trouble we get in, he can always get a good night's sleep.

Getana lay quietly beside him, also watching the bay. Jem walked a few yards of shell beach to the water's edge. He wondered where the big sea gull was as he paced nervously back and forth, splashing his feet in the tiny wavelets. Getana joined him suddenly and stood whining out into the dark.

"Ya hear somethin', don't ya girl?" Jem said in a low voice. But the dog only moved back up the beach a little and lay down.

The moon rose, flooding the bay with cold, pale light, and he saw them, five longboats headed north, four with their sails set and the fifth being towed. Without a doubt,

45

they were the same boats from the night before. As Jem watched, they changed course and headed directly toward him.

Getana rose, growling low, and might have barked if Jem had not quieted her. "Come on girl, we gotta get hid!" he ordered as they ran for the trees.

"Wake up, Raif, they're comin'!" he announced, shaking his friend awake. Raif was up in an instant and Jem pointed to the boats. "Looks like they're landin' on this end of the island."

They crawled far back under the low, spreading limbs of the cedars and waited. The boats hit ground while still some fifty yards from the island, and the men began cursing as they splashed about in the shallows, dragging the boats ashore.

The boys watched, hardly daring to breathe as the procession of dark figures dragged the boats to a spot nearby where the trees grew almost down to the water. The hacking of cutlasses and axes echoed across the island as limbs were cut for camouflage. Jem kept one hand on Getana and stroked her head every time she started to growl. Before long they saw the dim light of a hidden campfire flickering through the trees.

"We gotta get closer," Jem whispered and started crawling through the underbrush. Raif followed him, and Getana moved beside them silently. The campfire cast weird shadows on the trees as they inched their way forward.

The first voice they heard was speaking English. "That blasted rudder has cost us a whole night's travel. Do ya think your bloody lubbers can fix it tonight, so's we can make the bayou tomorrow night?"

The answering voice spoke with a strong Spanish accent. "Do not be concerned, Señor Vibart; it will be done in plenty of time."

"Aye, that's what ya was sayin' last night. I don't like stopping on Black Jack's Island. The place gives me the creeps just knowin' he used to come here. Kept a boat

46

hid somewhere on the island, he did. Used it once or twice ta get away from the Mexican cavalry."

As the boys moved closer, they could see that the man who spoke next wore the uniform of a Mexican naval officer. He had a huge black mustache, and the firelight reflected off a single gold tooth every time he spoke. "Had your ambush been better laid, then your 'Señor Black Jack' would be a ghost and you would be a much richer man."

"Nothin' but a dang piece of rotten luck, somethin' scarin' that sea gull like it did."

"What concerns me more than your fear of old memories, Señor Vibart, is the fact that, somewhere out there is someone who knows we are here."

"Your men said they were just kids."

The officer scratched his chin. "So it was said, but they called the girl by name and took a great risk to try to rescue her. That seems unusual for a couple of '*muchachos,*' I think."

"We best be disposin' of that little wretch. She's been nothing but trouble."

The officer shook his head. "The time to have disposed of her was when she first saw us at Hanna Reef."

"We covered our tracks good enough," Vibart insisted. "If anyone finds her skiff, they'll figure she fell overboard and drowned. And her dog's been fed to the fish. That girl ain't of no use ta us no more."

"I think it would be interesting to know who tried to rescue her. I suggest you persuade her to tell us."

Vibart nodded thoughfully and then yelled, "Lopez, bring the little wretch over here, and take care she don't bite ya no more."

Jem felt Getana move beside him as Talva was pushed into the firelight. "No! Not yet!" Jem whispered in her ear, and both he and Raif struggled to hold the big dog down.

The officer picked up a bowl of food from near the

47

fire and held it under Talva's nose. "You should eat," he said.

Talva ignored him and stood with her eyes downcast.

"It's no use. She won't eat nothin'."

The officer repeated his statement in Spanish.

"We don't even know if she can talk," Vibart complained. "We ain't heard her utter a word yet."

"Señorita," the officer said, kneeling beside her. "This *gringo* here wants to slit your throat and feed you to the fish. I believe that if you will tell us who tried to rescue you last night, he might be persuaded to keep you alive. Otherwise, I have no choice but to agree with him."

Talva ignored him, but as the boys watched, she raised her eyes slowly and looked around the fire. She seemed to be waking from a dazed sleep.

"She knows we're here," Jem suddenly realized. "She senses our presence."

"I will ask you once again," the officer said as Vibart drew his knife and tested the blade against his finger. "Who were the people who tried to rescue you?"

Talva looked at the blade and then up into the eyes of the Mexican officer. "Lafitte," she said, and the slightest hint of a smile crossed her thin face.

Jem almost choked as he realized she had told the truth but that *he* was the Lafitte she was referring to. Vibart, of course, thought otherwise. He took a full step backward and almost dropped his knife. "She's . . . lyin'," he stammered.

The officer shook his head. "No, I was looking right into her eyes as she spoke. I saw only truth."

"He wouldn't dare follow us. He only had two men with him."

Again the Mexican officer turned to Talva. "And what, little girl, are you to Jean Lafitte, or 'Black Jack,' as Señor Vibart insists on calling him?"

Talva gave him a sudden, wicked smile, "A friend of one who wears his locket with the black falcon."

48

The officer turned back to Vibart who was looking suddenly pale. "What is she talking about, this locket?"

Vibart was plainly frightened. "It . . ., it was his symbol of protection, given only to a handful of people in all the years he was in Louisiana and Texas. No one outside the Brotherhood of the Coast knew its meaning. I seen only one once, was around the neck of his last wife. Reckon she was wearin' it when they left the island."

Jem touched his locket. It suddenly felt very heavy.

"So then there is no question that this wretched little girl is telling the truth?"

"Maybe, but Lafitte would not be crazy enough to come after us with just two men," Vibart argued.

"But we do know that he took one of your boats from Bolivar Island and escaped into the bay before my landing party got ashore."

"So what? He's on the run somewhere. But we got twenty men; he'll be stayin' as far away from us as he can."

"Perhaps," the officer replied and then said to Talva, "Why does he want you so much?"

"You will know soon enough," Talva answered.

"If Señor Vibart has his way, you will not be alive to know what happens. I think you should tell us everything you know."

Talva just stared at him and said nothing.

The officer nodded. "I find you are very interesting. We will keep you around a while longer and watch you very closely."

8

With his pocketknife open and clutched in his right hand, Jem crept ever closer to the firelight. Five yards ahead he could see the tree to which Talva had been tied several hours before. Since then, Raif, Getana and himself had lain silently in the thick underbrush, suffering from ants and mosquitos while waiting for the camp to quiet down. Thirty minutes ago, they had seen only one man still awake and decided that the time was right. Now, that same sailor was nodding sleepily across the fire.

Every inch seemed like a mile as Jem carefully felt the ground in front of him for leaves or sticks or anything that might make a noise and give him away. Nearby, he could hear the uneven snoring of Vibart and others. His heart was racing, beating so hard that he was afraid it would wake the sleeping men. The excitement made him feel dizzy and short of breath, as if he had been running for miles.

Talva turned her head slowly, and for a moment

their eyes met. Then she motioned with her head toward the dozing guard. Jem nodded and crawled the last few inches. It seemed to take forever to cut the ropes that held her to the tree. Just as the last rope parted, the guard opened his eyes.

Jem flattened himself on the ground with his face in the dirt and Talva lowered her head, pretending to be asleep. Time seemed to stand still as the guard slowly got to his feet and walked toward them. He stopped in front of Talva and stood towering above her for a long time while Jem held his breath.

All seemed well, the guard thought. The girl was asleep; everything was fine. He returned to the fire and poured himself a cup of coffee from the pot which hung from a stick above the coals. He mumbled to himself something about checking the boats and disappeared toward the beach.

"Come on!"Jem whispered as Talva slipped out of the ropes and crawled toward him. In a few seconds they had faded into the night to become darting shadows, all running for the secret anchorage. The low shell bank appeared in front of them and they could see the *Falcon,* waiting for them. Raif tumbled aboard as Jem untied the bowline and threw it after him.

A single pistol shot froze them all in their tracks. A second later they could hear yelling and cursing from the camp. "Hurry, they are on to us! Raif whispered loudly as Talva climbed into the boat.

"Don't set the sail yet! They'd see it for sure in this moonlight. We'll row until we get out of sight," Jem said as he started to push off.

"Getana, come on," Talva called, but the big dog held back, growling and watching the trees. Jem left the boat and ran up the bank. He grabbed the dog by the hair of her neck and began pulling on her. "Come on, girl, we gotta get outa here," he whispered desperately.

There was a crackling of leaves in the underbrush and a dark figure stepped from the trees. Jem heard the ominous, hollow "click" as a pistol was cocked and saw one of the sailors standing above him.

Getana tore from his grip, pulling him down as she jumped at the dark figure. The pistol dropped unfired to the ground and bounced away unseen. Dog and sailor blended to look like a dark whirlwind, spinning in the moonlight. The sailor was screaming in Spanish above the sounds of tearing cloth and growling dog. In the midst of the battle he suddenly broke free and scrambled to his feet. He ran like a man pursued by a hundred devils but made the fatal mistake of looking back. He slammed headlong into the largest tree within a hundred yards of the cove. It brought him to an immediate halt, and he staggered in circles for a few seconds and then fell, face down onto the ground.

Getana returned, happily panting and wagging her tail as she jumped into the boat. Jem pushed the bow away from the shore and climbed aboard last. They pulled the *Falcon* past the trees and out into the bay. In the distance they could see the camp in total confusion. Someone had built up the fire for more light, and they could hear Vibart yelling, "Look to the boats, ya lubbers, they can't get off the island without a boat!"

"They think we are going to steal one of their boats," Raif snickered. "Boy, are they going to be surprised."

"I reckon that proves they don't know nothin' 'bout the secret cove then," Jem answered and kept rowing.

An hour later they had passed behind another low island and could no longer see Vingt-et-un. "Talva?" Jem asked. "Do you know someplace we can hide? Reckon they'll be hot after us come mornin'."

Talva had said nothing since her rescue. As soon as they were clear of the island, she had crawled up to the bow and sat with her arms tightly around Getana's neck. In response to Jem, she raised her head and seemed to take a long time to decide where she was. At last she pointed at the dark outline of Trinity Bay's eastern shore. "There, the place where the trees grow tallest. You will find the entrance to a bayou." She fell silent again and buried her face in Getana's long hair. A little later the boys could hear her crying quietly, and then she was asleep.

It was well after dawn when they found the bayou. A wet mist hung along the shore, and the sun shone as a dim, yellow ball just above the hazy outlines of tall pine trees. Water had eroded away the banks, leaving a tangle of broken trees and rotting stumps where shore birds watched silently as the *Falcon* drifted in on a dying wind.

Talva raised her head and pointed silently at a fork in the bayou which turned south. It looked narrow and even more desolate. They rowed the *Falcon* now, pulling slowly down the twisting stream.

An old chimney stood deserted and forlorn on a low hill beside the bayou. "What was that?" Jem asked as they passed.

"The ruins of some old cabin," Talva told them. "My mother said it was here when she came. It is a sad place. I never go there."

Around the first bend was a tiny, muddy island with one broken tree in its center. Talva pointed toward shore, and they nosed into a tiny channel which turned behind a grove of pines and ended abruptly.

"Why we stoppin' here?" Jem asked as their bow bumped the shore.

"It is my home," Talva answered. "We can eat and rest here."

Jem had many questions, but he felt that Talva was not ready to answer them yet. He only nodded his agreement.

"Well, I am certainly in favor of eating," Raif announced cheerfully. "I have forgotten when I had my last meal."

"Last night," Jem answered.

Raif thought for a moment and smiled, "Oh yes, I

guess it was. But, you must admit that it has been a very long night."

"Reckon I can't argue with that," Jem added as he stepped ashore. Getana was running in circles and barking, plainly happy to be home. But Talva remained quiet as she led them up a narrow path to a little cabin made of logs and mud. It was set in a tiny clearing, surrounded by tall pines. Above the doorway were several brightly painted symbols of stars, strange plants, and animals. When Raif stopped to study them, Talva said, "They are pentagrams. They keep away evil spirits."

"Will they keep away the Mexican Navy?" Jem asked sarcastically.

"They will help," Talva told him without emotion as they entered the cabin. Inside, the floor was made of hard-packed dirt which had become almost like concrete. There were three large windows, each of which could be closed with heavy wooden shutters. On the fourth wall was a fireplace with a stone hearth and beside it, a simple table, and one chair. Against the eastern wall was a small altar with two candles and a large book, which Jem assumed was a Bible. Beside it were a few shelves with bottles and jars. A narrow cot was against the north wall. A blanket decorated with symbols similar to those over the door covered it neatly.

Talva started a fire, then left. She returned in a few minutes with several fresh redfish on a stringer.

"Hey," Raif said. "That's the fastest fishing I ever saw."

"Do not be silly. I keep them in a trap in the cove," she said, and immediately started to cook the meal. Within an hour, they were feasting on fried fish, vegetables, and dried fruit.

When they had finished and nothing remained but the skeletons of four fish, Talva said: "There is much we must talk about and many decisions we must make. But I think we should rest now, and talk tonight."

Jem objected at first, but Raif reminded him that it had been almost three days since either of them had had more than a couple of hours of sleep. Without further protest, he dropped down on the floor and, using one of the food bags from the boat as a pillow, was soon fast asleep.

Jem awoke in the late afternoon feeling terrible. Every bone in his body ached. For the first time in days he realized just how tired he had been. Talva was sitting on the cot and staring silently out the window. Raif was just beginning to stir.

Jem drew a dipper of water from the bucket on the table and drank heavily. "Feel like I been drug around by the dogs," he said absently and sat down on the floor.

Raif sat up and Talva said, "We should talk now. There is not too much time."

Raif yawned and nodded his head in agreement. He sleepily asked "Was that your pet sea gull following us around the bay?"

Talva smiled. "Hardly. Mariah is no one's pet. He is King of Gulls. And like all good kings, he has many duties. But my mother healed his wing when he was young, and now he will sometimes help me."

Raif said, "I wish he had helped us a little more. We ran right into those boats in the middle of the night."

"You must understand," Talva continued. "I did not send for you because I needed to be rescued . . . that came later. I asked Mariah to find you because your father is in trouble, and we may be the only ones who can help him."

Jem jumped to his feet. "Where is he?" he blurted out.

Talva shook her head. "I do not know. I saw him before the Mexicans caught me. But this story should be told from the beginning."

"More than a month ago I went to gather herbs on Bolivar Island. One night when the tides were high, two dark ships anchored off Rollover Pass. From one of the ships many barrels and heavy boxes were brought ashore, and there were men from Galveston who met them. They carried everything across the island and loaded it into small boats. Then the ships put back to sea and the small boats sailed north past Hanna Reef and crossed Red Fish Bar near where you first saw the men who captured me."

"Sounds like smugglers," Raif commented.

"That is what I also thought. But just six days ago, I returned to Bolivar. The tides were again high. This time it was a different ship that anchored off Rollover Pass. It was smaller and its masts were raked, but it carried many cannon." She paused and looked straight at Jem. "Your father came ashore from it."

Jem's mouth dropped open and he started to ask something, but Talva silenced him. "Let me finish," she insisted, and then recounted the ambush and fight which had taken place on the beach.

"Then what happened?" Jem asked anxiously when she had finished.

"His ship made sail and ran for the open sea when the two Mexican warships appeared. Your father and his two friends, the fat one and the big one, crossed the island and escaped in one of the boats brought by Vibart's men. I sent Mariah to find you, and I followed them.

"By then one of the other ships had landed men, and Vibart had told them what happened. They loaded the remaining boats and also headed north. I heard cannon fire far out at sea, but I do not know what happened to your father's ship.

"The wind was strong and the boat your father took was much faster than my skiff. In the morning, the Mexicans caught up with me near Hanna Reef. The one called Vibart said I might tell someone they were here, and so they took me with them. They sank my skiff and threw Getana overboard. Later, they camped in some trees along the shore and sailed again that night. That is when you first stumbled onto them."

"I still can't figure what they're up to," Jem said.

Talva sighed gravely. "That I learned while I was their captive. The Mexican Army is going to invade Texas."

Raif frowned. "I doubt that. And even if they were, what would they be doing up here?"

"They spoke of their president, Santa Anna, who fears the Texas Navy more than anything else. He remembers well the damage that was done to his supply ships before the Battle of San Jacinto and also the beating they gave the Mexican fleet off Yucatan just last year."

"So they're smugglin' all their supplies in before they get here?"

"Yes, Jem, they are hiding them somewhere up one of the bayous north of here. When the time is right, soldiers will also land at Rollover Pass and follow the same route. Then they will be in position to attack wherever they choose."

"Wow!" Raif exclaimed. "We better get back to Galveston real fast and tell the Army!"

Jem shook his head. "Who'd believe us? We're just a couple of kids, and we ain't got one lick of proof."

Talva agreed. "He is right, and besides, there is another problem. Jem's father is somewhere up here also."

"What is he doing here, anyway?" Jem asked next.

"From what I could learn from listening to the men,

59

the Mexican government sent a message to your father at someplace called 'The Isle of Pines' and offered him a great deal of money for his help with their invasion."

Jem's heart was in his mouth as he waited for her to continue.

Talva paused and smiled slightly. "Instead of helping. He has been attacking their ships. I think the one they call Vibart used to sail with your father. Lately, he was your father's agent in Galveston, but he is a traitor. He sold out to the Mexicans. Since there is still a reward for your father, Vibart set up the ambush on the beach."

Now it all made sense, Jem thought. But what to do about it? That was the question.

"I still think we should get back to Galveston and tell somebody. After all, what can three kids do by themselves, 'specially when one of those kids, namely *me,* isn't going to have anything to do with another crazy scheme?" Raif said.

Jem ignored him. "If we could find my father, he'd know what to do."

"Can we do that?" Raif asked. They both looked at Talva.

The girl turned away and stared out the window. "I do not know."

"You found us pretty easy," Jem encouraged her.

"It was Mariah who found you, not I."

"But ain't you a . . . I mean you can feel things like—"

She turned on them suddenly. "You mean am I a witch?" She shook her head. "I do not know. But if I am, I am surely not a very good one or I would never have been caught by those men." She rose from the cot where she had been sitting and walked to the small altar against the cabin's east wall. "My mother left me her instruments," she said, touching the book, and Jem realized for the first time that it was not a Bible. Written in silver across its ancient, leather cover was *The Book of Shadows.*

"Aw come on, Talva, ya gotta do somethin'."

The girl nodded. "You saved my life. That is a debt

60

that a witch does not take lightly. I will do what I can." From beneath her cot, she removed a small knapsack, made from a burlap bag, and carefully placed *The Book of Shadows* and several other items from the altar into it. "Stay here tonight. I shall return in the morning."

"Where ya goin?" Jem insisted on knowing.

"To a special place in the forest. A place where spells are cast and spirits are called. A place you must never see."

"A place this kid does not ever want to see and does not even want to hear talked about," Raif assured her loudly.

She reached the doorway and Getana rose to follow. Talva's eyes stopped her without a sound, and the dog laid down with her head on the floor. "Magic has an odor she can smell and knows to stay clear of," Talva said and disappeared into the gathering twilight.

Raif lit a single candle sitting on the table. He shivered as it cast dancing shadows across the cabin walls. Then he said, "Our friend Talva is sure a strange girl."

"Yeah, I hate just sittin' here all night."

"True, but I was more afraid she was going to tell us we had to come with her."

Darkness surrounded the cabin. The tall trees lining the bayou's banks hid the stars and made the night pitch black. Jem walked to the door and stared out. If there was any wind, the forest blocked it completely. Not even the insects were making noise.

Too much had happened for Jem to remain content, waiting for morning. The excitement of the past days still pounded in his head. He felt closer to finding his father than he had ever felt before. But the darkness weighed him down, stifled him like some black hood being forced over his head.

"Maybe we should follow her," he suggested with a sudden grin.

"Of all the crazy things I have ever heard come out of your mouth," Raif exploded, "that is the worst idea you have ever had! I do not even want to think about what she is doing."

"Reckon I'll have to go alone then."

"Go alone? You have got to be kidding! I am not going to stay here alone, and I am sure not going off in the dark following Talva."

"Aw come on, you ain't scared, are ya?"

Raif looked indignant. "Of course I am scared. And maybe if I stay that way, we might all get out of this mess alive. But that has nothing to do with it. Whatever Talva is doing, she has to do it alone. Besides, it is darker than sin out there. We couldn't follow anyone if we had to."

Jem considered that statement and realized that, of course, it was completely correct. "Reckon I'll just go for a walk then, you want to come?"

"No, but I suppose I will because I do not like this spooky old cabin any better than I like the spooky old dark night."

Outside the cabin, the boys cautiously followed the pathway back to the Bayou's edge. As their eyes slowly adjusted to the darkness, they found that they could see a little. They could barely make out a pathway leading along the bank and followed it.

Every low bush looked like a crouching animal as they tiptoed along. The bayou beside them was a pale strip of light, winding through the dark shadows of the forest. The path ended abruptly at a tiny point of land. Just ahead, they could barely make out the old chimney silhouetted against the dark sky.

Raif touched Jem's arm and pointed at the water. There was a longboat being rowed up the bayou. "It must be the Mexicans coming after us!" Raif whispered as the boys ducked behind the nearest bush. "We better get out of here; they are going to pass right by us."

"I don't think it's the same men," Jem told him. "It's just one boat."

"I think you are guessing when you should be running."

62

"Just don't move and they won't see us."

The boat pulled ever closer, and Jem realized that his feet were almost in the bayou. The boat would pass within a few feet of them. The silence became deafening. Although the boat moved swiftly, there was no sound of oars being pulled through the water and the sail was clearly furled.

"I do not like this!" Raif whispered near panic. They both held their breath as the boat glided past within a few feet of their hiding place. Two men were rowing, but there was still no sound. A third was in the bow and a fourth stood at the tiller, deftly guiding the silent craft through the darkness. For a moment, the figure passed through an opening in the trees and was silhouetted against the night sky. Jem focused on one of the men. His features were hidden beneath a heavy cloak, but Jem could see that he wore a wide-brimmed hat with one side pinned up. He had seen it once before.

Jem opened his mouth to call out, but Raif's hand covered it before any sound escaped. Jem was furious and tried to kick at Raif as the boy pushed him down even lower behind the bushes and sat on top of him. When he at last broke free, the boat had vanished in the night.

"Dang it Raif, what'd you do that fore?" Jem demanded hotly.

Raif was astonished. "What did I do that for? I thought you were about to sneeze or cough or something. I did not know what, but whatever you were going to do, it was going to make noise and the Mexicans would hear it and be right on top of us. So, of course, I stopped you."

"Dang it all!" Jem cursed and threw a handful of dirt into the water. "That wasn't the danged Mexicans; that was my father!"

10

"Your father!" Raif exclaimed. "Well, why did you not say so?"

"Cause you was holdin' me down tryin' ta suffocate me, that's why!" Jem scolded.

"I do not see how you could tell who that was. In fact, I think our eyes were playing tricks on us and that whole boat was not even real."

"Now that's plumb crazy."

"Then why couldn't we hear them rowing?"

Jem sighed, " 'Cause they had their oars muffled. It's an old pirate trick for sneakin' up on anchored ships. Ya wrap cloth around the oars and then they don't make any noise."

"Oh," Raif answered thoughtfully. "Well, come on then, maybe we can catch up to them." The two boys hurried along the path, bumping into things in the dark. But they found so sign of the mysterious longboat. As the path faded out somewhere past Talva's cabin, they gave up.

"I think they were movin' too fast for us," Jem said as they walked back to the cabin.

"Yes, and if we had caught up with them in the dark, they might have accidentally shot us," Raif added.

Disappointed, they returned to the cabin. The rest of the night passed with neither of the boys getting much sleep.

Talva returned an hour after sunrise looking very tired. "We must go north and look for signs," she said, before either Jem or Raif had time to tell her about their night adventure.

"My father ain't north. We seen him go up the bayou last night," Jem protested.

Talva looked confused for a moment and then nodded. "I see. Then we will follow this bayou. I had a vision of your father at a place where two bayous join, one big and one small. I believe it was to the north. I have never followed this bayou very far, but I have always believed it turns north and might join Double Bayou."

"And what are we supposed to do when we get there?" Raif wanted to know.

Telva only shrugged. "There, we will find what it is we seek."

Raif was not convinced. "Hey Jem, are we really going off into that swamp just because Talva had a vision?"

"Nope, I'm goin' 'cause that's the way I seen that longboat headin' last night. Reckon it don't hurt none that her vision happens to agree with me."

"I still think we should get back to Galveston and tell the Army what is happening."

Jem finished throwing a few more things into a bag and then stood up. "If you want to, Raif, take the *Falcon* and sail back to Galveston."

"You'd trust me with the *Falcon?*" Raif sounded astonished.

"I reckon there ain't no sense in all of us takin' the chance."

"We should all go together," Talva insisted.

Raif released a long held breath and sighed. "All

65

right, we will all go together, but I am sure that I am going to wish I was back in Galveston."

They rowed the *Falcon* up the winding bayou all that morning. A light mist shrouded the banks and made the trees look fuzzy in the morning sunlight. The bayou narrowed and wound its way beneath a towering canopy of trees that kept out the sun and left the bayou in a world of twilight and shadows.

Lacy ferns, still sparkling with dew, lined the banks. Beyond them, the forest floor was a misty carpet of earth-scented moss and dead leaves. Jem felt very small. The trees seemed to him as if they reached all the way to the sky. An occasional long-necked bird watched them from the banks, and black cormorants dove into the bayou's muddy water as they passed. Once they thought they saw a fleeting deer vanish into the forest, but mostly, there were only the sounds of the oars and of water rippling past the *Falcon's* hull.

In an hour or so, the bayou opened out onto a stretch of marshland dotted with only a few large trees which clung to high places along the bank. Tall marsh grass grew so high that they could not see more than a few yards.

"I think we've turned north," Jem said, looking over his shoulder at the sun. No one agreed or disagreed with him.

By noon, the bayou was again entering a grove of trees which appeared to stretch far away into the distance. Almost as soon as the *Falcon* was under the trees, the bayou became very narrow. Ahead, they could see it was choked with vegetation.

"I don't think that longboat could have gone much farther," Jem said as his oar struck the mud bottom.

"Then it must be somewhere nearby," Talva commented, looking along the bank for someplace a boat might be hidden.

"Maybe there?" Jem pointed and turned the *Falcon* toward the bank. At one place, the bushes seemed to have

66

been crushed, and as the bow touched ground, they could see a fresh rut in the soft bank.

"Looks like they dragged the boat ashore here," Jem announced as he stepped onto the shore and started walking into the weeds. Then yards ahead, he fell over the longboat's stern.

"I found it!" he called out, and in a few seconds his friends had joined him. They pulled off the covering of limbs that had been left to hide the boat and looked inside. The mast had been removed and laid along the port gunwale. Beside it, the sail was neatly furled. Beneath one of the seats were two large jugs of water and a small leather bag filled with dried meat. Two cutlasses were also stowed under the seats.

Raif lifted one of them and was amazed at how heavy it was. "Hey now," he said, brandishing the weapon awkwardly. "Bring on those bullies!" With that, he advanced on the nearest tree and hacked off several branches with unsteady strokes. On his last stroke he missed the tree, and the weight of the cutlass carried him down into an ungraceful seat on the ground.

"Beware of the terrible pirate," Talva laughed. Getana barked and soon they were all laughing. Before long they decided it was time for lunch. Talva spread the old tarp from the *Falcon* on the ground, and they all sat eating dried fruit. Talva produced another bag. "The Indians call this 'pemmicen.' It is made from deer meat and suet, ground into a paste, and then pressed into these little cakes." She handed each of the boys one. "Eat only one. They are very filling and will last you a long time. It is said that an Indian warrior can run all day on just one of these."

Raif examined his cautiously and sniffed it before taking a bite. "I think this kid would need many more than one of these to run all day. Of course, I do not have any intention of running all day. I am not even that fond of walking all day."

"Speakin' of walkin'," Jem sighed, "I reckon we better be figurin' out which way we go next."

"I do not see any sign of a trail," Raif observed, looking at the thick forest which surrounded them. They all began to carefully survey the area.

Jem spotted the tracks first. They were only faint impressions in the dark earth, but he was sure there were four different sets of them.

"Three of 'em are wearing boots. Fourth one must be wearin' something like moccasins 'cause there ain't no mark for a heel."

"Talva," Jem asked, "Didn't you say there was just two men with my father?"

"Yes, I am sure of that."

"There were four men in the longboat we saw last night and there are four sets of tracks here."

"I heard your father say something about still having a friend or two on this coast. Perhaps one of them has joined him."

"Here are some more tracks," Raif announced, poking under some weeds.

They are still going north," Jem said. "Now all we can do is follow 'em."

Jem returned to the boats. "Come on," he said, "let's hide the *Falcon*. Then we'll take just what we can carry and get moving."

With some difficulty, they dragged the *Falcon* up onto the bank and hid it beside the longboat. Into Talva's knapsack went most of the food and a blanket she had brought. Raif volunteered to carry it first. Talva also had brought a goatskin canteen which they filled and Jem slung over his shoulder.

"Shall we take the cutlasses for protection?" Raif asked as they started to leave.

Jem lifted one and held it in his hands. Despite its weight, it felt strangely at home there. He was trying to make up his mind when Talva said, "One of them might be useful in cutting our way through the thick woods."

Jem agreed, and they argued about which one they should take. In the end, Raif and Jem both carried one.

The afternoon moved slowly as they followed the faint tracks northward. Time and again they would lose them on hard ground and then have to walk in wide circles until they picked them up again. Once, when they lost the tracks completely along a low rise, it was Getana who picked up the trail. Occasionally, they saw glimpses of the bayou to their right and knew that the trail was running more or less parallel to it. As the shadows of evening became longer and the soft light on the forest floor began to fail, tracking became even harder.

"I wonder how far we have come?" Raif asked, as again they spread out to try and find the elusive tracks.

"Seems like we bin walkin' forever. But I don't think we've gone very far," Jem told him.

"And we will not go much farther tonight," Talva added, looking up at the sky through the treetops.

"Yeah, it'll be dark soon. We should find a place to camp."

"I do not like this place at all. Everything is damp, and I have seen two snakes already today," said Raif.

Talva raised one eyebrow and frowned at him. "Do not bite the snakes and they are not likely to bite you."

"Let's keep movin' for a while longer. looks like there might be some higher ground up ahead," Jem suggested, pointing north.

A half hour later they had reached a low rise crowned with several large oak trees. The bayou, although narrow and choked with vines and fallen trees, ran close beside it. Raif immediately set about building a fire.

"I don't think we oughta build a fire. We don't know how close we are," Jem said.

Raif was plainly disappointed. "Yes, and we do not even know *if* we are close, or what we might be close *to,* if by some chance we are close to *anything,*" he grumbled. He stopped preparing the fire and took out another of

Talva's pemmicen cakes, eyeing it sadly. "Well, my little friend, it is just you and me," and with that he took a large bite.

Darkness came quickly deep in the forest, and there was little for the three adventurers to do except try to sleep. The night was cool, and Jem wished that they had brought more blankets. Sometime before moonrise, he dropped off into a restless sleep.

He awoke scared. The moon was high and the forest floor spotted with little pools of pale light. Above him, the tree branches were swaying in a light wind.

A musket shot echoed through the night, and he realized that it had been another shot which had awakened him. Jem jumped to his feet as another shot and then another rumbled far in the distance. Then there was a rapid volley of gunfire which echoed like thunder, and afterward, a strange, ominous silence.

11

"*Madre Maria,*" Raif whispered in the deathly silence. "It sounds like the whole Mexican Army is already here and the war has begun."

"I think it came from the north," Jem said uncertainly.

Talva doubted it. "How can you tell where it came from? Everything echoes in the forest."

"I ain't sure, but we gotta get there fast." Jem fumbled for their few belongings in the dark.

We should wait for daylight," Talva insisted. "We will only get lost in the dark."

I think she is right," Raif agreed quickly. "We might fall in a big hole or something."

Jem found himself outvoted, so they waited impatiently for the first sign of morning. There was little more than a dim glow beyond the trees when they started out. The forest was shrouded in a gray fog, which made the trees look as black as coal. Dewdrops hung on every leaf and branch. There was no wind, and not a single bird sang.

Raif asked, "How do we know we are still going the right direction? I have not seen any more tracks since last night."

"We don't know," Jem admitted. "But I ain't got any other ideas."

Talva added, "We can only follow the bayou now." And so they kept the narrow band of muddy water in sight, afraid they would lose their way if they strayed far from it.

Suddenly, Getana growled softly and pressed against Talva's side. They all stopped and listened but heard nothing. The forest remained silent and lurking.

Jem took the lead and moved forward, watching carefully to avoid any branch or leaf which might give them away. Slowly, they made their way up a slight rise where the forest became choked with a thicket of thorns and brambles. Getana growled again as Jem began to work his way around the thicket in the direction of the bayou. The bank sloped down gently beneath a low but thick covering of vines.

Jem moved cautiously, placing each step so as to remain silent. Had he been moving any differently, he would never have seen the pistol which lay entangled in the brush.

He picked it up carefully as Raif and Talva moved close beside him. "Been fired," he observed, seeing that the hammer was down and the flash pan open.

"It must have been dropped by someone in that fight we heard last night," Raif added as he touched the weapon and then quickly drew his hand away. "And I think the owner did not fare so well." Raif was staring at a streak of half-dried blood across his hand which had come from the pistol.

"There is more," Talva said, pointing at a trail of reddish brown drops which led toward the thicket. Getana sniffed the trail and whined. "It is odd," she added. "She no longer seems afraid but is now eager to follow. As if . . . " She left the statement unfinished as they followed Getana toward the thicket.

Jem lifted his heavy cutlass and held it in front of him with both hands, but it quickly tired him and he rested the blade on his shoulder. It was so heavy that he began to wonder if he would be able to swing it in a fight.

Raif pointed to Getana and whispered, "It seems like she smells somebody she knows."

The dog wiggled her way beneath some vines on the thicket's edge as the three young adventurers hurried after her. They crawled on their hands and knees for a few yards until the thicket opened up into a small clearing covered from the sky by a canopy of branches.

Lying face down in the center was a body.

"Madre Maria," Raif gasped as he crawled into the clearing, "it is a dead man."

Getana was whining and sniffing the body, nuzzling her nose beneath one arm.

"Perhaps he is not dead yet, " Talva suggested.

Raif said quickly, "Well, I am not going to turn him over to find out." The figure wore a pair of ragged canvas pants and a loose-fitting shirt, which seemed to be more patches than shirt. A red bandana was around his head, and a single gold earring hung from one ear. A rusty cutlass lay beside him.

Memories flashed across Jem's mind. It had been over a year ago, in the ruins of the old pirate fort at Galveston. Two seamen with clubs had cornered an old man that everyone called "Crazy Ben." When Jem had joined the fight, they were intent on beating the man to death to learn where he had hidden some coins. The old man's knife had taken one of them just as Jem had used the only weapon he had. His brick had sailed on an arc-shaped course and bounced with a satisfying thud off the remaining seaman's head. The attacker's club had dropped to the floor and his hand went to his temple. For a second, he had looked blankly at Jem and then collapsed.

74

The man they called "Crazy Ben" had turned quickly, seeing Jem for the first time. For a few confused seconds, he had leveled his knife in Jem's direction and the world had stood still as they faced each other. Then a crooked smile spread across the scarred face, Crazy Ben had touched the knife's hilt to his chin in the traditional dueler's salute, and then replaced it smartly in his belt. "Get out, lad, there's likely more of 'em about," he had said and then vanished somewhere among the ruins.

When they had next met, it was months later and they were far up on Clear Creek. Ben had become their friend and partner in last summer's treasure hunt. Besides Raif and Talva, he was the only other person who knew the secret of Jem's father.

Jem was shaking, and there were tears in his eyes as he turned the body over and stared at the scarred face.

"It's Ben!" Raif exclaimed from behind him. "What's he doin' here?"

Talva was kneeling beside him, touching his neck with her hand. "I think he still lives."

"Can ya help him?" Jem asked, trying hard not to cry.

"Perhaps," Talva whispered as she examined a dark stain of dried blood which covered his shoulder and spread down his arm. "He has been shot, but I think the ball went completely through."

"Is that good?" Raif looked sick.

"Better than if it had stayed inside to poison him."

"So there's a chance?" Jem asked.

Talva only nodded and tried to give him a drink from the goatskin canteen. They wrapped Ben in the only blanket they had brought. Talva made a gooey mixture of mud and tree bark along with the leaves of a plant Jem had never seen before. She applied this to the wound and then dressed it with a bandage cut from a strip of the blanket.

A million questions rambled through Jem's mind. The last time they had seen Ben was last summer. He had lived up one of the bayous that emptied into Clear

Creek. As near as Jem could tell, that was at least fifteen miles by boat from where they were now. It seemed certain that he must have somehow been involved in this whole mystery, but Jem could not figure how Ben could have known about it in the first place.

"You think that Ben also might have seen those boats moving at night and followed them here?" Raif asked in a whisper.

"I don't know, but I reckon it's got somethin' ta do with the Mexicans invadin'."

Raif snapped his fingers. "You know, I remember one of the men saying something about Ben, that night on Vingt-et-un."

"I also remember that," Talva agreed. "Vibart said that he was watching the bayous to the west and that he would not be a problem."

Ben showed some sign of life during the afternoon. One eye opened, and he seemed to recognize his friends. Talva gave him a sip of water, and then he coughed and said, "Well, me young friends, ya be the last faces Ol' Ben was expectin' ta see again."

"You should rest now," Talva told him.

Ben shook his gray head. "Ye've got ta get away from here; there's trouble up the bayou. Ye be in great danger — " Ben coughed and tried to continue.

"You have said enough," Talva insisted. "You must rest now." Ben took another sip of water and closed his eyes. In a moment he was again resting peacefully.

"We still do not know if your father is here or not," Raif said thoughtully.

"He's here!" Jem answered stubbornly.

"Perhaps he can tell us more when he has rested for a while," Talva said.

"You reckon he'll be all right?"

"It would be better if we could build a fire, but I do not know if it would be safe."

"I been thinkin' about that," Jem answered. "I reckon Raif an' me better scout up ahead and try to find out

76

if there's still any Mexicans around." Talva nodded her agreement.

Jem and Raif considered taking the cutlasses with them, but both agreed that the swords were so heavy they would probably be of no use to them in a fight. Leaving them sticking in the ground, the two boys set out saying they would be back by dark.

They had walked for less than half an hour, keeping the bayou close on their right, when Jem heard brush cracking in the distance.

"Somebody's coming," he whispered.

"Yes, and out here it is not likely they will be friends."

The two boys ducked behind the nearest available cover, which happened to be a fallen tree that was rotten and almost hidden beneath forest vines. Again there was the cracking of some branches. They raised their heads just enough for their eyes to peer over the log as a shadow moved beside the bayou.

Before they could tell anything about it, a second shadow detached itself from the forest a few yards away from the first.

"Mexican sailors again," Raif whispered in Jem's ear.

There was more noise to their right, and other figures appeared through the trees.

"Yeah, a bunch of 'em. The way they're all spread out, they must be lookin' for somethin'."

"Yes," Raif's voice was urgent. "And I think it is us they are looking for."

"More likely for Ben."

"Oh, that is just fine! And now what are we going to do? They are soon going to be all around us!"

Jem knew he was right. Desperately, he looked for some route of escape and found none. Whatever way they moved, they were sure to be seen.

"Reckon the only way is down," Jem whispered and

began to burrow his way down among the vines which nearly covered the old log.

"I suppose it is better than just sitting here," Raif agreed. He also began to cover himself with vines. In a few moments, they were both lying close alongside the old log, peering through a patchwork of grass and vines.

Jem was almost afraid to breathe as the footsteps came closer and closer, crunching on the forest floor. A huge black boot stepped over the log and came down inches from his nose. A gruff voice said something in Spanish, and for an instant he believed he had been discovered. The butt of a musket came to rest on the ground beside the boots as a Mexican sailor sat down on the log.

Jem held his breath until he almost turned blue. When he finally did breathe in, the odor of tobacco was strong and he could see the man filling a clay pipe with tobacco from a leather pouch.

A bug began to crawl up Jem's ankle, tickling him with each tiny step it took. Jem gritted his teeth as the insect marched confidently onto his thigh. He wanted desperately to move, to brush the insect away, but he barely dared to breathe.

Other voices were all around him, speaking Spanish. Everywhere, he could hear the clumping of boots on the forest floor. An eternity seemed to pass before the sailor seated above him finally got to his feet and picked up his musket. Another eternity passed before the patrol began to move off down the bayou.

At last Jem breathed a sigh of relief. Cautiously, he raised his head above the vines which had concealed him and looked around. Beside him, Raif was doing the same thing.

"That was too close for this kid. I thought they were going to step all over me."

"I counted at least a dozen of them," Jem said as at last he swatted at the pesky insect beneath his pants.

"What do we do now? They are headed in the direction of the thicket where Talva and Ben are hiding."

Jem watched the last figure vanish into the forest. "We better not follow 'em." They got to their feet, brushing off leaves. "Let's head on up the bayou and maybe we can find out where they came from."

There was a sudden movement behind them, and as they turned, a cold voice stopped them in their tracks.

"Well, now, a pair of ragamuffins raising up from the ground. What da ya think, Lopez, maybe they be some sort of foul weeds growing out here."

"I think they are in a lot of trouble, Mr. Vibart."

12

"So what do we do with 'em, Mr. Vibart?" Lopez asked as Vibart scratched his chin thoughtfully.

Before Vibart could speak, Raif started talking. "Hey, we sure are glad to see you. We have been lost for two days and we cannot find our way out of this forest. We are two starving little kids. You got anything to eat?"

"You're lyin'. There ain't a soul livin' within ten miles of here," Vibart growled.

"You mean we came all that way? Wow, I thought we were probably walking in circles. Hey, you hear that, Jem, we must have come over ten miles. Man, we sure did get lost."

Vibart was ignoring Raif's rambling. His eyes had become suddenly fixed on Jem's locket. "Blast me eyes, Lopez," he hissed between his teeth, "If I didn't know better, I'd say that be a — "

The sentence went unfinished as Raif suddenly charged at Lopez, butting him in the stomach and knocking him to his knees. Jem took the cue as their only chance and pushed Vibart as hard as he could. Vibart took one step back, trying to retain his balance, and then fell over Lopez who was just getting to his knees.

"Run for it!" both boys yelled at the same time.

Jem ran with no thought of which direction he was going. He could hear Raif puffing along behind him. Branches scratched his face and tore at his clothes as he charged headlong through the woods. Somewhere a shot rang out and then another. One ball whined safely above him, but a second slammed into a nearby tree and sent splinters flying off in all directions.

Jem skidded around a big tree and ran headlong into a Mexican sailor. He felt a big hand grab at his collar and tear it almost completely from his shirt, but he managed to break away.

"Over this way!" he heard Raif yell some distance away. When he turned, Raif had vanished and there were two sailors less than ten yards behind him. There was no time to think or hesitate; he could only keep running, as fast as his legs would carry him.

Behind him was a steady crashing of brush as the sailors continued the chase. Two other shots rang out, but this time they were farther away and he heard no balls whine past him.

Jem's heart pounded until he was sure it would burst, but still, he kept running. The forest opened up slightly in front of him as he sprinted down into a small depression where the leaves lay deep and the ground beneath them was muddy. Then, the ground rose sharply and beyond it was a wide bayou, bordered by oak trees. Jem halted and looked behind him. At least two men were still chasing him, although they were now some fifty yards behind.

Desperately, he looked for some route of escape. To his right the ground was open. The sailors, with their longer legs, would run him to ground quickly there. To the left was a thicket. There, he might hide for a while, but sooner or later they would flush him out.

That left only the bayou. "Uncle Moss told me once that most sailors don't know how to swim," Jem remembered. "Sure does look cold, but I reckon it's better'n gettin' caught."

He took one more look behind him and then flung off his shoes and dove into the dark water. Jem went deep, clawing his way to the muddy bottom and swimming as fast as could in the same direction as the current.

During the summers at Galveston, Jem had often dove for lost articles dropped from the wharf or from aboard some ship. Usually he could stay down for about two minutes, but now he was so winded that he seemed to need air almost before he had reached the bottom. The cold water chilled him instantly, making him shake all over as he swam toward the surface. When his head broke water, the first things he saw were tree roots.

Blinking the muddy water from his eyes, Jem realized that he had surfaced beneath one of the big oaks which grew close to the bayou where the current had eroded away the bank and left most of its roots exposed.

Jem hung on, catching his breath while keeping his head barely above the surface. He could feel the bayou's current gently tugging at him, trying to pull him from his hiding place. In the distance were voices, and he heard footsteps along the bank above him. He tried to hold his breath again put only managed to do so for a few seconds.

"You think the little nipper drowned, Mr. Vibart?" He was sure it was Lopez's voice.

"Maybe; maybe not."

There was a rasping noise as if someone was poking along the bank with a stick. A shiny flash of steel stabbed between the roots and passed inches in front of his nose as he realized that they were probing for him, and not with a stick, with a cutlass! Jem took one deep breath and dove for the bottom, using the tree roots to pull himself down.

Seconds dragged by as Jem fought to hold his breath.

He was shaking uncontrollably, shivering until his teeth chattered in the cold water. At last he could endure it no longer and came to the surface. Around him was only stillness. He could barely hear voices as the men continued to search for him further downstream.

"Nothin' ta do now but just hold on and stay right here 'till dark," Jem thought. And then where would he go? He had no idea. He was now totally lost. This bayou, he was sure, was much too wide to be the same one they had been following. Also, he wondered what had happened to Raif. The last he could remember seeing of him, he had still been running. He could only hope that he made it back to warn Talva. But, even if he had, what good would it do? They could not move Ben, and so they would have to remain hidden and hope.

Night came slowly along the bayou. A light fog clung to the water and colored the trees with an eerie gray. Jem crawled cautiously from the water, feeling like a drowned rat. For a while, he sat huddled at the base of the tree in whose roots he had been hiding.

A long dark shadow drifted down the bayou. At first Jem thought it was a log and watched as it drifted closer and closer to him. It was only a few yards away when it suddenly opened its mouth and Jem realized that it was the biggest alligator he had ever seen. It turned toward him then, and Jem quickly began to climb the oak tree. His wet hands slipped on the branches as he heard the alligator climbing onto the bank behind him. Jem wiggled one leg over the lowest branch and kept climbing until he was well off the ground.

"Dang it," he whispered as he sat perched like a big wet bird in the tree, "now even *I* wish I'd stayed home." But instantly he knew that he was not telling himself the truth. If he had not come, Talva would still be a prisoner and Ben would have died for sure. He also realized that unless he did something pretty soon, none of that would matter.

Everything had gone wrong, and Jem thought that

83

most of it was his own fault. Perhaps they should have done as Raif suggested and returned to Galveston to warn the authorities. It had been a foolish idea to come here.

He looked at the North Star and decided that the bayou ran east and west. Talva had said they should go to a place where Lone Oak Bayou joined another Bayou. This must certainly be the other bayou.

The moon rose and began its slow climb into the night sky as he pondered his next move. He wanted to try to return to the thicket. If Raif had managed to escape, then he would head back there; that is, if he did not become just as lost as Jem now was.

A shadow crossed the moon and Jem looked skyward. A bird circled lazily above the bayou and then dove suddenly down toward the tree in which Jem was sitting.

"I wonder . . .?" Jem started and then there was a sudden rustle of wind as the big sea gull landed on the limb beside him.

"Mariah!" Jem almost shouted. "I reckon I'm glad ta see you, even if it seems like there's always trouble when you show up." The bird ignored him and began cleaning its beak on the tree. "Reckon you could have a talk with that gator down there?"

The bird did nothing, but Jem looked down and could no longer see any sign of the alligator.

"I gotta find Raif and Talva. Which way do I go?" A long moment passed before the big sea gull finally flew up into the air. He circled the tree once and then flew off east along the bayou.

Jem climbed carefully down out of the tree, still keeping an eye out for the alligator, and started walking. "Reckon I was really lost. This is 'bout the last direction I figured to go to the thicket again."

Moonlight cast weird shadows among the trees as Jem moved cautiously along the bayou. Frogs were croaking near the water's edge and mosquitos buzzed in

84

his ears. Walking warmed him somewhat, but his wet clothes were cold and clammy. His shirt stuck to his skin.

He waded a small stream which emptied into the bayou and froze halfway across as something moved in the forest not far away.

"Probably a deer," he told himself and kept moving but wondered if it might be another alligator — or something worse.

By the time the moon had begun to sink in the western sky, Jem was beginning to wonder if he had made a mistake in following the sea gull. He was certain the thicket where he had left Talva and Old Ben would not have been this far away, and it would have to have been farther to the south. But now he was uncertain of any other way to go, and so he continued to drag himself along the bayou's bank, keeping close enough to its edge so as not to lose his direction.

Several more times during the night, he heard things moving in the forest near him, and he wondered if there was something out there stalking him.

Jem fought to stay awake. He had considered finding a place to sleep until dawn but decided against it. It would be better to go as far as he could while he still had the cover of darkness.

Pausing on a little rise, he blinked his eyes at the forest ahead and thought for one moment that he had seen the dim glow of a fire. He looked again, straining his eyes, but saw nothing.

A limb snapped somewhere to his right, the same sound he had heard several times before during the night. Jem looked for cover. To his right was what appeared to be a large bush, big enough to hide under. Jem ran for it and dove beneath it.

His head hit something hard, and for a moment hundreds of little stars danced in his brain.

"Dang, this ain't no bush," he whispered as he explored this new object with his hands. There were branches there, but they had been cut and were dead and dry. Beneath them he felt the familiar texture of sail-cloth.

"Canvas," he thought and wiggled his way beneath it. The next thing he touched was hard, made of wood, and banded with iron.

"Barrels," he whispered, "But barrels of what?" There was a whole stack of them, at least two dozen, Jem guessed. His hands explored the end of the closest one, and his fingers picked up traces of a grainy powder. He pressed it close to his nose, sniffed at it, and then touched it to his tongue.

"I ain't sure," he whispered to himself, "but I got a bad feelin' that I'm hidin' under enough gunpowder ta blow a hole from here back ta Galveston."

13

Footsteps crunched on dry leaves and Jem held his breath. They stopped just inches from where he sat hidden beneath the canvas and pressed against the powder kegs. It seemed like forever before they began to move away.

Jem lifted a corner of the tarp and peered out into the gray light of dawn. Walking away from his hiding place was a Mexican sailor. There was a cutlass in his belt, and he carried a long musket on his shoulder.

"Looks like I found where the Mexicans got their arms hid all right," Jem thought. "Now if I just had any idea what I could do about it — "

His thoughts were suddenly interrupted by the rustle of some leaves behind him. Someone else was very close. He dropped the canvas back in place and squeezed between two of the powder kegs. Holding his breath, he waited. There was a scratching noise and a little light spilled in as one edge of the canvas was lifted a few inches. Jem could just see the toe of a leather moccasin and two big hands feeling for the end of one of the kegs. They were so close that they almost touched his foot.

As he watched, the hands pulled the wooden stopper from the keg, let a little of the gray gunpowder spill onto the ground, and then stuck a long piece of cord into the opening.

Darkness again shut out his vision as the canvas was dropped carefully back in place. Outside, there was a click, followed by a quiet pop, and then he heard footsteps running away.

For a moment, Jem sat still, trying to figure out what was going on. He was still guessing when he smelled smoke. He lifted the corner of the canvas and was confronted by a wisp of gray smoke coming from the end of a piece of slow-burning fuse.

"Somebody's fixin ta blow this place up and me with it," he realized and immediately looked for someplace to run. But dawn had almost broken. He could see men crawling out of their blankets. Beside them, not more than twenty yards away, someone was stirring the coals of a campfire. The forest was too open to the rear, and in front was the Mexican camp. A clump of low bushes appeared to be almost fifty yards away, and he was considering trying to crawl to it when he noticed there was already someone behind it. Jem blinked his eyes and looked again.

There was a huge man there, crawling on his stomach toward a fallen tree which lay a little farther away. The man was bigger than any two of the Mexicans put together, and he wore moccasins. As Jem watched, the man stopped long enough to cock the hammer of a blunderbuss and then slipped out of sight behind the fallen log.

"That must be the man who lit the fuse," Jem thought, "but who is he?"

Jem took another quick look at the fuse and guessed it had perhaps a minute left to burn. He looked back at the fallen tree and wondered if he could get to it without being seen. There was more movement there. Two more heads appeared for a moment above it. His heart skipped a beat when he saw that one of them wore a wide-brimmed hat which he had seen before.

He remembered a night on the beach at Galveston, over a year ago. That same figure had stood watching him from atop a sand dune, silhouetted against the moon. It had been the night before someone had mysteriously completed the repairs on the *Falcon,* which allowed him to begin his treasure hunt. And again, just two nights before, that same figure had been in the longboat which passed him and Raif on Lone Oak Bayou.

"Father?" he whispered. The word sounded strange to his lips. But suddenly it all became crystal clear. Talva had said there were two men with his father when she saw them on Bolivar Island. It must be that they were now trying to do the same thing which had brought Jem here. They were going to attack the camp and destroy the supplies stored here.

"Dang it all," he whispered. "If I run now, I'll give the whole attack away and get everybody killed." He shot the fuse another desperate look.

"But if I stay . . . " The answer was painfully clear. A cold chill went up Jem's spine, colder than the bayou water had been last night and colder than any fear he had ever known before.

There were more footsteps beyond the canvas. "The guard again," Jem thought, as a musket was set down inches away from his feet. His fate was sealed. Now there was no escape. If he ran, the guard would shoot him. If he stayed, he would be blown to bits.

Only the steady hiss of the fuse behind him broke the stillness. The strong, acid odor of burning powder stung his eyes, and he wanted to cough.

The guard outside was mumbling something. He sniffed loudly and then flung open one corner of the canvas. Jem squeezed himself tighter between the kegs and sat frozen, waiting for the guard to see him. But the guard had other things to worry about. He cursed loudly in Spanish and then grabbed at the fuse, flinging it away onto the ground. Jem was sure that in another second, the guard would see him. Then he would probably shoot him, and it would all be over. He had failed in everything he had set out to do. He thought of Raif and Talva and hoped they had escaped.

A distant voice was yelling in Spanish. Was the alarm already being sounded?

There was something familiar about the voice. It was the same voice Raif had used when he had fooled the boat's crew that night near Hanna Reef. Jem was not sure just what he was yelling, but it was something about coming quick.

The guard grabbed up his musket and ran toward the camp. Jem breathed a momentary sigh of relief and then realized what he must do. The powder still had to be destroyed. He would have to replace the fuse. With grim determination, he scrambled from between the kegs and spotted the smoldering fuse still hissing on the ground a few feet away. It looked terribly short. Only an inch or two was left as Jem grabbed it up.

"I reckon here goes nothin'," he said as he stuck the fuse back into the open powder keg. And then he ran, ran like he had never run before in his whole life. The explosion picked him up and hurled him forward. Branches and patches of sky revolved in his blurred field of vision. Grass and roots hurried by him in a blur. There were other explosions. Bright flashes of light lit up the forest like midday. Shots rang out through the spinning forest; they sounded far away and echoed on the rolling thunder of the explosions.

Jem hit the ground hard and rolled against a tree. For a minute he felt dizzy, and the world refused to stop spinning. As he staggered to his feet, his head hurt and the forest still spun in lazy circles. There was a huge, smoking hole where the powder had been.

Jem strained to focus his burning eyes on the fight which was now going on in the camp. His head hurt terribly, and something warm was running down his forehead. He saw his father in the midst of the fight, a sword in one hand and a smoking pistol in the other. On his right was the big man who had first lit the fuse, and to his left was a short, round man with a double-barreled pistol in each hand. Wisps of gray powder smoke drifted over the scene. Men were falling everywhere. Out of the smoke, the man they called Vibart was running at his father with a bared cutlass in his hand. As Jem watched, his father parried the blow and drove Vibart's blade into the ground. His own sword flashed in the first rays of morning sun, and Vibart went down heavily. But others came at them, pressing their attack from all directions.

Jem started running toward the fight, but the world seemed to be in slow motion. The trees passed him by as if he were walking, his legs felt as if they were carrying a great weight, and it was all he could do to lift them. Ahead, he could see the battle with a strange, unreal clarity as if it had been painted with bright, glowing paint. It seemed to Jem as if he would never reach it. No matter how far or how fast he ran, his father was always still just beyond his reach.

The morning sun seemed to spin in lazy circles as it retreated faster and faster down a long tunnel until there was no light left, and he remembered nothing more.

14

Jem came to his senses amidst a tangle of thorny vines. At first he thought it was raining, and then he realized that something wet was being rubbed across his face.

"Cut it out," he mumbled. 'I don't want no bath now.'

"Be still," he heard Talva say from somewhere beyond his foggy vision. "I cannot tell how badly you are hurt."

"I'm all right," Jem insisted, groggily and sat up. "What happened?"

"I fear that *you* must tell *me*. From the look of things, I think you destroyed the Mexican camp and most all of their supplies."

Jem blinked and tried to focus his eyes, but the forest remained a spinning blur. "My father, is he all right and Raif?"

"I have seen neither of them. Were they here?"

"Gotta find 'em," Jem groaned and tried to stand. His legs felt like water beneath him, and he immediately fell.

"If they were here, they are gone now," Talva insisted.

"He was here. I saw him. He attacked the camp. Raif, too."

Talva sounded suspicious. "Raif was here too?"

"I heard him yelling something in Spanish."

Talva looked doubtful and handed Jem her goatskin canteen. "Drink," she said. "And then we will go back to the thicket where Ben is resting."

"You left him there?"

The girl nodded. "He is better. I left Getana with him and followed you when I heard the explosions and shooting."

Slowly Jem's head cleared, and he found that he could stand and could walk, although every step hurt. With Talva's help, they walked toward the remains of the camp.

Everything seemed to be destroyed. Broken muskets and pistols lay scattered about along with blankets, clothing, and other gear. There were several large holes where other powder caches had exploded. The cooking fire was still smoldering, and a pot lay overturned in the coals.

"Are they all dead?" Jem asked as they moved cautiously around the bodies of two Mexican sailors.

"All that are here. I found Lopez and also the Mexican officer. There were several explosions. I think that is what killed most of them. I saw several which had been shot and heard some more off them running through the forest."

"What about Vibart?"

"I have not seen anything of him."

"I seen my father kill him. They was right about here, I think."

Talva frowned at him doubtfully again but said nothing. Just beyond the camp, a small cove was formed where the two bayous joined. Five longboats were still

94

there, pulled up onto the muddy shore and covered with branches.

"None of 'em got away in the boats," Jem observed. "And that means they're still out there in the forest somewhere. We gotta be real careful."

"Maybe we could bring Ben here and use one of these boats to get him out," Talva suggested.

"I reckon that's a good idea, 'cept for one thing. My father's gonna be headed the other way, back ta Bolivar where his ship will be lookin' for him. If I go out by boat, I'll never see him."

"Would you let a friend die, just to meet him?" Talva glared at him, her dark eyes suddenly aflame.

Jem glared back at her for a moment and then turned away. "There's gotta be another way," he said pleading. "Maybe you could take Ben out in the boat while I stay and — "

Talva was pointing at the heavy longboats. "I could not even drag one of those to the water. And if somehow that could be done, then I would not be strong enough to row it. Together, we could step the mast and sail her, but alone, it would be impossible."

"At least we gotta find Raif first," Jem insisted.

"He will try to return to the thicket, if he is able. We could wait there at least until tomorrow morning."

Jem nodded his head and fought back his tears as he gripped the longboat's gunnels with both hands and tried to stop himself from shaking.

Talva's hand touched his shoulder. "Raif is smart; he will be all right. And your father, it seems as if fate has chosen some other time for your paths to cross. For now, there are still two friends who need your help."

Jem looked at her, not understanding.

"Ben, and me," she said smiling and quickly turned away.

Jem watched her as she picked up one of the Mexican blankets from the ground along with another canteen and one of the cooking pots. "Ya know," he said, "you ain't like none of them girls back in Galveston."

Talva followed him as he walked back to where the body of one of the Mexican sailors lay on the ground and picked up a hat which lay nearby.

"What do you want with that?" Talva asked.

Gotta have some kind of proof that all this really happened. Ain't nobody gonna believe me in Galveston."

A long knife also lay beside the dead sailor, and Jem picked it up also.

"It is a strange knife," Talva said.

"Called a 'dirk.' He was a midshipman." Jem glanced up at Talva who plainly did not understand. "That's what I always wanted to be in the Texas Navy. They start 'em real young, twelve years old sometimes. I don't reckon he was much older than me. Regular swords are too big for 'em, so they carry one of these."

Jem unbuckled the dead midshipman's dirk and placed it in his own belt.

At last they left the battle site and started back toward the thicket. The forest was silent as they walked keeping close to the weed-choked bayou. Talva had picked up some dried meat and a sack of beans in addition to the small cooking pot and two blankets from the destroyed camp. She offered some of the dried meat to Jem, but he refused it.

"You have not eaten since yesterday," she scolded.

"Ain't hungry."

"We have many miles to go, and you look as though you are already half dead."

"Said I ain't hungry."

Talva sounded disgusted. "Must you be as foolish as you are stubborn?"

"I ain't stubborn, and you're actin' like some old mother hen."

Talva stopped and stood for a moment on the trail as Jem walked away. Then she shook her head and followed him.

96

15

"Something is not right," Talva said in a whisper as she touched Jem's arm to stop him. Ahead was the thicket where they had left Old Ben and Getana. "We are downwind; Getana should have smelled our scent by now."

She cupped her hands carefully over her mouth and gave a short whistle which sounded to Jem exactly like the call of a morning dove. It was answered only with silence and the faint rustle of wind through the trees.

"Ben couldn't move by himself, could he?" Jem asked.

Talva shook her head, "I think not."

"Jem thought for a moment and said, "We can circle around and sneak up from over there." Talva nodded, and Jem led the way as they moved cautiously around to the east side of the thicket where the trees were larger. The forest remained deathly silent and, no matter how carefully he moved, each step seemed to echo loudly.

They crawled behind a fallen tree and peered over it. There was still no sign of life in the thicket. Again, Talva called in her strange, birdlike whistle. Again, there was no answer.

A shadow fell suddenly across the log, and Jem felt movement behind him. He spun around in time to see Vibart standing over them. The man's eyes were red and wild with rage. Dark stains of half-dried blood were spread over his torn shirt and down one leg of his trousers. His left arm was clutched to his side, but in his right hand a heavy cutlass was raised over his head. Even as Jem turned, it was starting down.

The air whistled with a savage scream as Jem rolled out of the way, and the shiny blade flashed past his ear. It sank into the log, inches between himself and Talva, throwing chips of rotten wood in all directions.

Jem was on his knees and crawling as fast as he could when the next slash passed over his head and clipped a small branch. He rolled away again and this time came up on his feet with his back against a tree. In the distance, he could see Talva and realized she was safe for the moment.

Vibart was facing him, towering above him and panting like a madman. "The Black Falcon!" he gasped in a half-crazed whisper. Vibart's bloodshot eyes were focused on the locket as if he were seeing a thousand ghosts from his own past.

"Blast my eyes if you're not Lafitte's own kin," Vibart's voice hissed snakelike between crooked yellow teeth as his eyes moved to Jem's face. "So Ol' Black Jack had a son. Well, that's fine and dandy it is. It'll be givin' me all the more satisfaction when I cut off yer head and leave yer bones for the gulls ta pick clean!

"Ye ruined it, ruined it all! The Mexicans would have made me rich," Vibart rambled aimlessly as Jem carefully drew the midshipman's dirk from his belt. "I was ta be governor of all of Galveston when they took Texas back. And now look at it. You blowed up everything, ruined all their guns, ruined — !" The cutlass swung in a wide slash as Jem ducked and darted away.

Vibart charged after him like an enraged bull. Again the cutlass flashed at him, and he raised the dirk. The heavy blow jarred every bone in his body, but he managed to hold onto his weapon and parry Vibart's blade away. The cold ring of steel against steel echoed among the trees. Vibart lunged, and again Jem darted away. The cutlass caught for a second on his already torn sleeve, ripping it away as he stumbled and retreated once more.

Jem backed into another tree, so tired now that he could barely hold the dirk. "Run, Talva, get away from here," he gasped, noticing that the girl was still a few yards away.

Vibart's cutlass was raised above his head. Jem gripped his dirk and braced himself for the blow which he feared would be the last. He wondered if he had even enough strength left to lift his weapon, much less parry the blow.

"Monsieur Vibart?"

The voice was cold and strange, yet somehow familiar. Vibart hesitated, his cutlass still raised above his head as if frozen in time. "Perhaps you would care to fight a somewhat larger Lafitte?"

Jem could see Vibart's face go suddenly pale. He turned slowly, his cutlass still raised above his head as if suspended in time. Four figures were standing not more than twenty paces away.

On the left was the huge giant of a man who had first lit the fuse to the powder kegs just that morning. The blunderbuss he carried looked as small as a pistol in his huge hands. On the right was a portly little man with a big smile and a bright red sash around his broad middle. He carried a brace of double-barreled pistols. Between them, they were supporting Ben.

Raif was there also, standing with his thumbs hooked under his suspenders and smiling from ear to ear as if he had personally arranged all of this.

Jean Lafitte stood in the center. Three times before,

Jem had seen fleeting glimpses of him. He had felt his presence, his guidance many more times. Now for the first time, he could see his face clearly. He was tanned by the southern sun to the color of fine leather. His hair and mustache were gray, but there was still a spark of fire in his dark eyes. A French rapier with a gold hilt twitched nervously in his hand.

Vibart broke the silence. "I'm wounded, Lafitte. I cannot fight you with a sword."

"The choice of weapons is of no concern to me," Lafitte said evenly. "There is a pistol in your belt. Feel free to use it if you wish."

Vibart's eyes brightened at the prospect as he clung to this sudden chance at survival. "By the code of the Brotherhood of the Coast, I call fair fight," he challenged and wiped a trickle of spit from his mouth.

"It is done," Lafitte answered him calmly as the others backed away. "There will be no interference, not now or when it is over."

Vibart stepped over a fallen log and into the open as Lafitte drove his rapier into the ground and moved away from it. Vibart's right hand hung nervously in the air for a second, and then he grabbed at the pistol. Jem saw him raise it clear of his belt and point it at his father's chest. Powder flashed in the priming pan, and Vibart's arm jerked with the weapon's recoil as gray smoke and fire belched from its muzzle. Vibart fell backward over the log and lay still.

Jem saw his father lower his own smoking pistol and replace it in his belt. As the ringing in Jem's ears died away, the first thing he heard was Raif.

"Hey, Mr. Lafitte, that was real good shooting, but as I told you, I think Vibart was really too scared to hit anything. Why he was shaking all over and — "

Talva grabbed his collar. "Raif," she said quietly, "be quiet or I shall turn you into a frog." She turned him away from the others and added, "I think we shall take a

100

walk now. You may tell everybody what a hero you are later."

The others were also backing away, and in a minute Jem stood alone facing his father. For almost a year he had thought of what he would say when, and if, this moment ever came. Many different things had crossed his mind, but now, none of them seemed right. It occurred to him that his father looked almost as dirty as he must look himself.

"Reckon my Uncle Moss would skin me alive, if I was ta come home lookin' like this," he said and realized that it had absolutely nothing to do with the situation.

"I suspect he would skin us both, and with good reason," his father answered. "No doubt we both look like something which has just crawled out of the bilges."

Jem fumbled with the dirk he still held and finally got it back into its sheath. "Took this dirk off one of them sailors. He looked ta be about the same age as me. Uncle Moss says I'm thirteen. That right?"

Lafitte seated himself on a log beside him and nodded. "You were born on July 4th, 1831. On an island called Isle Mujeres. It is off the coast of — "

"Off the coast of Yucatan by just a couple of miles," Jem interrupted. "I seen it on a navigatin' chart once aboard a collier brig. We was mendin' topsails on her."

"Your friend Raif told me why you came here. You know it was a very dangerous thing to do?"

"Talva sent word to me, said you were here somewhere. Once we got started, I reckon things happened kind of fast."

"And you did well. I think we would have failed if you had not replaced that fuse. And Ben would surely have died if you had not found him."

"Dang it all!" Jem suddenly exploded, "Why did you just go away last summer? I could of gone with ya!" At last it all began to come out, all the long pent-up anger and frustration. "Wern't right ta hide from me and then

101

run off!" Jem was on his feet, his hands knotted into tight fists at his side. "It wasn't fair!"

His father's eyes bored into him as he said, "You will never know how hard it was for me to leave without you. But, do you know what my head is worth in Mexico today?"

Jem shook his head.

"Enough gold for most men to live quite well for the rest of their lives. In England and Spain, of course, the reward is considerably higher."

"Reckon that means I ain't goin' with ya this time either."

Lafitte sighed and shook his head. "There is some question now as to where I am going. But if I can get back to the coast in time, my ship may return for me. If it does, then it is likely that I will be sailing into another fight before very long."

"I'm a good seaman," Jem argued. "I can fix sails, an' Uncle Moss says he'll send me ta sea with a captain ta teach me all about navigatin' and stuff just as soon as I'm fifteen. Seems like it might as well be on your ship."

"My ships are still at war with Spain and England and also Mexico. When it is over, I would be most proud for you to sail with me. But for now, it cannot be."

"Reckon I knew that . . .," Jem started to say, but his tears blinded him and the sentence went unfinished. Before he knew it he was in his father's arms.

16

The campfire burned low, casting strange, ghostly shadows among the trees which grew so close together that only a few stars managed to twinkle through their lacy canopy of branches. The aroma of beef stew, made from dried meat, boiled and seasoned with wild herbs and peppers, drifted over the small group of adventurers.

"It was all quite easy, Jem," Raif was explaining. "I met up with Mr. Lafitte after we got separated. Of course, I recognized him right away and then I helped him figure out how we should attack the Mexican camp. You see my friend, the whole plan hinged on my creating a diversion by speaking Spanish to the guards and telling them there was a big attack coming from up the bayou. That gave your father and his men plenty of time to blow up the gunpowder caches and destroy the arms."

"How'd you know he was my father?" Jem asked.

Cochrane was seated beside Ben with his back against a tree calmly sharpening his cutlass with a stone. "Simple it was," he said suddenly. "We told 'im just as soon as he woke up."

"Woke up?"

"Aye, Master Jem, the little nipper ran flat inta me and knocked hisself out cold, he did."

Everyone laughed except Raif, who suddenly began to shrink down inside his shirt.

"That is of no matter," Lafitte said to Raif. "We are most grateful for your help. Without it we would not have known Ben was still alive. And we would not have returned to the thicket in time to surprise the late Mr. Vibart."

The one called Fat Jack added with a laugh, "And without young Raif there, that fine dog would have eaten us all before we ever got close enough to Ben to move him." He pointed at Getana who was lying with her nose very close to the cooking pot.

Talva sighed as she stirred the stew with a stick. "Was it really necessary to tell him all that? Now I fear his head has swelled so badly that he will fall over when he tries to walk." Again the camp resounded with laughter. Raif blushed.

"I reckon I still don't understand how Ben got here in the first place," Jem wondered.

"On Bolivar, I heard you say that you still had a friend or two along this coast. I suspected then that you meant Ben," Talva said.

Lafitte nodded. "Quite right. I never completely trusted Magnus Vibart."

"You an' me both, Cap'n," Ben broke in, shifting his bandaged shoulder to a more comfortable position. "He came ta see me last fall, said there might be a Mexican invasion comin' anytime. Told me that he was your secret agent in Galveston and for me to watch for any sign of boats moving up Clear Creek. Well now, it didn't seem likely ta me that anybody sneakin' 'round Galveston Bay would come up the west shore. There be just too much traffic over there, what with the steamboats running up ta Harrisburg from Galveston nearly everyday. Ol' Ben figured he best scout over round Double Bayou an' Vingt-et-un.

"I spied their boats slippin' over Red Fish Bar one night 'way last month and knew fur a fact there was somethin' goin' on up the bayou here."

Lafitte continued the story. "When we took one of Vibart's boats, we sailed immediately for Clear Creek to find Ben. Of course, he told us what was happening and so we followed. Ben knew that Double Bayou could be reached by following Long Oak Bayou, so we came that way.

"When we stumbled onto one of the Mexican patrols in the dark and Ben was shot, we believed he was dead. We were not sure what we were going to do when Raif ran into Cochrane there."

Supper was soon ready, and they all ate heartily with barely a word among them. When the meal was finished, Talva asked, "Vingt-et-un is a strange name; what does it mean?"

"In French, it is the number twenty-one. But it is also the name of a card game which, in English, you call 'Black Jack.' Many years ago, some of my men gave me that nickname. I was never very fond of it, but since I used that island sometimes, the name has stuck to it all these years."

It was Fat Jack who spoke next. "Ya know, Cap'n, we've still got a bit of a problem about gettin' out of here."

Lafitte nodded. "Quite right. If the *Pride* is able, she will be cruising close off Rollover Pass in two days time. We will be hard pressed to all get there."

"You must take Ben back to Clear Creek," Talva insisted.

Cochrane doubted it could be done in time. "Them longboats is too slow if ya ain't got a dozen bully boys ta pull the oars on 'em."

Lafitte scratched his gray mustache. "If one of us could get to Rollover Pass by day after tomorrow, we could meet the *Pride* and arrange another time to pick up the rest of us."

"And that would give us time to take Ben back home."

Jem's eyes suddenly lit up. "The *Falcon* could get ta Rollover Pass by tomorrow night if there's any wind a'tall. Heck, she sailed circles around them longboats when they chased us that night off Hanna Reef!"

"A good plan," Lafitte agreed. "I will sail with Captain Jem and meet the *Pride*." He turned to Fat Jack. "Can you and Cochrane get Ben home in a longboat and then sail on to Rollover Pass if I give you one week?"

"Aye, Captain," Fat Jack nodded. "We'll take young Raif with us to help row. And then we'll drop him off at Galveston as we pass."

Lafitte shifted his gaze to Talva. "And what of you, young lady? You and Getana have been a great help to us. Is there anything we can do in return?"

Talva thought for a moment. "Vibart sank my skiff. I must find some way to replace it. Without a boat, I cannot fish the bay or gather eggs or even find oysters. I would take one of the longboats, but they are too heavy for me to handle."

Old Ben spoke up. "Come with us to Clear Creek and as soon as I'm up and about again, Ol' Ben will build ya the finest sailin' skiff what ever plied this bay."

A rare smile spread across Talva's thin face. "And I shall repay you by being your nurse until then."

"Then it is settled. We will leave at first light," Lafitte said. Only a few glowing embers burned in the fire as they settled down for the night.

"You know," Lafitte said thoughtfully just before they went to sleep. "I'm not sure how we would have found the Mexican camp at all if it had not been for that big sea gull which kept flying around over it and making noise."

Jem looked at Raif who in turn looked at Talva. They smiled at each other and kept that one secret to themselves.

106

17

Jem and his father had said their goodbyes to the others just before dawn. They had almost left before Jem remembered that he still carried Talva's cross in his pocket. "Reckon I'll see ya sometime. Raif an' me might go cruisin' come summer."

She smiled at him as he piaced it over her neck. Then she kissed him on the cheek. "Take care, my special friend," she said.

Jem had blushed such a deep red that he was sure his face must have glowed in the dim light. Fat Jack had laughed and nudged Cochrane in the ribs. "Like father, like son, they says. Blast me if there was ever a Lafitte born who was not a fine one with the ladies."

Jem could not remember ever being so embarrassed. But now as he thought back on it, being kissed was not really all that bad. And, after all, it would probably never happen again.

It was well into the afternoon before they had reached the place where the *Falcon* and the other longboat were hidden on the bank. It had taken another few minutes to step the mast and bend on her sails.

Jem steered a steady course as the *Falcon* sailed easily along Lone Oak Bayou with both her mainsail and jib filled by a southeast wind that somehow managed to find its way through the tall oaks and cedars which clung to the bayou's banks.

His father sat comfortably in the bow, apparently quite satisfied with the *Falcon's* limited space. "You handle her well, my son," he said.

"She's a good boat," Jem answered proudly. "Reckon there ain't nothin' her size in the whole bay that can catch her lightin air."

They talked of many things. Jem learned that he had an uncle whose real name was Alexander Lafitte but who was known all through the Caribbean as "Dominic Youx." He had fought alongside Jem's father at the Battle of New Orleans and commanded the cannon which turned the tide of that battle and ended England's last attempt to reconquer America.

They passed the little cove where Talva's cabin stood hidden among the trees and made the last turn before the bayou opened up into the bay. Jem was looking at the lonely old chimney he had seen when he had passed here before. It seemed like a very long time ago now, but Jem realized that it had been less than five days.

"I still reckon I ought ta be goin' with you," he announced.

His father did not answer at first. Instead he pointed at the old chimney and said, "Put her into the shore. There is something here that you should see."

Jem started to ask, "what" but noticed a faraway look in his father's eyes. He turned in toward the shore, freed his jib sheet, and eased the bow onto the muddy bank. Together they pulled the *Falcon* a little further out of the water.

"What's here?" Jem asked as he looked around and saw nothing but tall weeds.

108

"This way," his father answered and started walking toward the old chimney.

Jem could see that there had been a cabin here many years ago. The chimney now was all that stood, but among the weeds were a few charred timbers.

"Reckon it burnt down," Jem said idly, but his father did not answer. When Jem looked up he was some distance away. Jem followed and found him standing over two narrow graves. Each had once been marked with a simple wooden cross. Now the crosses had fallen over and rotted almost completely away.

"Your grandparents," Lafitte said softly.

Jem looked up at his father, totally taken by surprise. "They lived here?" he asked.

"It was here that I met your mother." His tone changed suddenly, and he turned away. "She helped me escape from the Mexican cavalry when one of my ships was sunk out there in the bay." He stared out across the water for a long moment and then continued. "When the Mexican soldiers found out she had helped me, they killed her parents and burned their farm."

"Why'd you tell me this?" Jem asked.

His father turned back suddenly to face him. "Perhaps I am trying to tell you why you cannot go with me."

"I don't understand . . ."

"Of all the things I have loved, it seems that you are the only one left. I would rather know that you are safe here than risk losing you by taking you with me to the places I must go."

Jem could see no hope in arguing any more. He kicked at a piece of wood and said, "I reckon Uncle Moss couldn't hardly get by if I was ta leave now," he said trying to smile. "What with all the ships comin' an goin' these days, it'd take him too long ta train anybody else."

The *Falcon* sailed south that afternoon and nosed into the secret cove at Vingt-et-un just after sunset. They camped on the beach and sailed late the following morning. It was noon before they crossed Red Fish Bar and laid a course to keep Hanna Reef to starboard and land them just west of Rollover Pass.

At sunset the *Falcon* was tacking into Little Pasture Cove, and within the hour she was beached among the marsh grass on the shore of Rollover Bay.

They lit Jem's old lantern and covered it with its shield, then walked across the sand dunes until they could hear the pounding of the surf in the distance. On the last line of dunes, they waited and watched the sea.

Above them the stars shone so brightly that Jem felt as if he could reach out and touch them if he tried. The group of stars Talva had called Orion were slowly crossing the sky to the west when the waning moon rose.

They felt the presence of the ship almost before they saw it, for it carried not a single light. The moon cast a pale glow on her sails and revealed a sharp, knifelike silhouette sweeping in close to shore. She was beautiful in a scary sort of way, Jem thought; so sleek and fast with her raked masts and the long line of bristling cannon showing along her side.

His father rose to his feet and removed the shield from the lantern. Quickly he flashed a signal, and it was answered by a tiny pinpoint of light from aboard the dark ship.

Her long bowsprit swung sharply into the wind, her sails popped and snapped loudly as she hove to. Almost before she had stopped moving, they could see a boat being lowered over her side.

"Well, my son, it is time," Lafitte said and pointed to Jem's locket. "Keep it close. As you have seen, there are still some who know its meaning." He paused and added, "Take care of yourself."

Jem fought back his tears. "Will I ever see you again?" he managed to say without choking.

"In my heart, I feel that there will be a time for us someday; someday when all of the wars are fought and deeds are done. For now, I suspect you are going to have a very hard time explaining to Uncle Moss where you have been for the last week or so."

The longboat was riding in over the white, glowing breakers. Lafitte set down the lantern. "Farewell, my son. We shall meet again." He extended his hand and Jem shook it. For a moment, they embraced, and then he was walking down to the waiting longboat.

Jem watched through tear-clouded eyes as the longboat pulled briskly back toward the waiting ship and vanished in the shadow of her swaying hull. Her sails filled as she turned off the wind and headed quickly out to sea.

Jem stood alone on the sand dunes until the ship was only a tiny speck on the moonlit sea. Then he picked up the lantern and started walking back toward the bay. There was no reason now for him to tell anyone about what had happened. It would be one more secret he would have to keep.

He suddenly missed Galveston and Uncle Moss and mending sails. He quickened his pace as he came down off the sand dunes and saw the *Falcon* in front of him.

"If I sail all night, I can be home pretty early tomorrow," he said to himself as he waded out and climbed aboard.

It felt good to be heading toward home.

Glossary

Anahuac: The oldest town in Texas. Established as a Spanish fort in 1821, it lies in the northeast corner of Galveston Bay near the mouth of the Trinity River.

anchorage: any area of protected water where ships may anchor

astern: behind or toward the back (stern) of a ship

bail: to remove water from a boat

barkentine: a three-masted sailing ship with square sails on the foremast and fore-and-aft sails on the main mast and mizzen

beat: To sail as close to the direction of the wind as a sailboat will go. Usually, this is at an angle of about forty-five degrees from the direction of the wind.

bilges: the lowest part of the inside of a ship or boat where water gathers

blunderbuss: A short single-shot weapon, similar to a shotgun with a bell-shaped muzzle. The name was derived from the old German word "donderbus" which means "thunder box."

boom: a spar which extends from the mast to the aft end of a sail and keeps it extended

bow: the front end of a boat

bow line: any line connected to the bow

bowchaser: a cannon mounted aboard a ship which is placed so it can fire forward, over the bow

bowsprit: a long, tapered spar extending forward of a ship's bow

brace of pistols: two pistols, usually carried in a wide belt

brig: a sailing vessel with two masts which carries square sails on both masts *caches:* places where food or supplies are hidden

canvas: a coursely woven cloth made of hemp or cotton, often used to make sails and tents

cast net: a fishing net, usually round, which is thrown out over the water

collier brig: a ship used to haul coal

Campeche: Jean Lafitte's pirate community located on the east end of Galveston Island from 1819 to 1821. It was named aftor a port on the Yucatan Coast which was also a hangout for pirates.

clear for action: The actions taken to prepare a warship for battle. This would include loading and running out cannon, rigging of boarding nets, shortening sail, clearing away of any unnecessary gear and many other actions.

compass: an instrument for finding direction which uses a magnetic needle that points to north

cormorant: a large, dark-colored, diving sea bird with webbed toes

corsair: any privateer, pirate, or sea raider

cutlass: a heavy sword with a curved blade, built for fighting aboard ship

dirk: a knife with a short, straight, pointed blade

docks: places to unload ships

Drinking Gord [Gourd]: an old southern name for the Big Dipper, a group of stars which rotates around the North Star

flash pan: the part on a flintlock firearm where the priming powder is ignited by sparks from the flint.

frigate: a medium-sized, fast warship usually with only one gundeck

furl: to drop and tie up sails

gaff: a short boom which holds out the top of a sail

ghost: to sail slowly in calm water when there appears to be no wind.

grapeshot: a cluster of small iron balls fired from a cannon

gunnels: Also called gunwales. The upper edge of a boat's hull. Originally, these were walls built as protection for guns.

gunports: openings in the side of a ship through which cannons are aimed and fired

hilt: the handle of a sword or dagger

hull: the body of a ship or boat

hoist: to lift or raise aloft

jib: a small, triangular sail usually flown from the headstay

keel: the main timber which runs the length of the bottom of a ship or boat

lagoon: a shallow lake or pond, usually connected to a larger body of water

lee: the side away from the wind

leg-o-mutton sail: Also called a sprit sail. A sail rig using a single sail and a spar connected near the base of the mast and extending out to the upper, rear edge of the sail.

longboat: the largest boat carried aboard ship

loose footed: a sail which is not attached to a boom

lugsail: a four-sided sail attached at the top to a single yard which is hung from the mast.

lugger: a small vessel equipped with a lug sail; once commonly used to unload anchored ships when no dock was available.

Maison Rouge: French for "Red House." The name given by Lafitte to his walled fortress on Galveston Island.

mainsail: the sail set from the largest mast on a boat or ship, usually the largest working sail

mast: the large, upright spar stepped on a boat's deck or keel to which the sails are attached

mooring lines: any rope or cable used to secure a boat or ship to a dock

midshipman: a student in training for the rank of lieutenant in the navy

musket: A single-shot, smooth bore weapon fired from the shoulder. It is less accurate than a rifle because it does not have grooves in the barrel which cause the bullet to spin.

Orion: A group of stars which resembles a hunter with bow and arrow. It rises in the east, sets in the west, and can by used for finding direction at sea.

parry: to turn away or deflect a blow

pentagram: a five-sided magical symbol, once believed to ward off evil spirits

port: the left side of a ship as seen when facing forward

rail: a narrow, wooden piece running along the top of the ship's sides

raked masts: masts on a ship which are slanted to the rear for more speed

rapier: a slender, two-edged sword, usually with a large, cup-shaped hilt

reef: a dangerous ridge of coral, rock, sand, or oyster shell lying just below the surface of the water

rudder: a flat, movable piece of wood at the stern of a boat which extends below the surface of the water. It is turned by the tiller or wheel and used to steer the boat.

sailor's palm: a glove-like piece of leather used to protect the palm of the hand while sewing sails

sandpiper: a small shore bird with a long, soft-tipped bill

scabbard: a sheath or case, usually attached to the belt for carrying a sword or knife

schooner: a type of sailing ship developed in America. Originally, schooners had two masts of which the foremast was the shorter. In later years, schooners were built with as many as six masts.

Sirius: the brightest star in the sky; appears to follow Orion across the night sky

skiff: a lightweight, narrow rowboat

slow match: a slow burning fuse used to fire a cannon

spoonbill: a wading bird with a broad, flat bill which is spoon-shaped at the tip

starboard: the righthand side of a boat as viewed by the helmsman

116

stem head: the top of the main timber at the bow of a boat to which the planks are fastened

stern: the rear or after part of a boat or ship

swivel gun: A small cannon mounted on a swivel. These were commonly used for arming small boats and for mounting along the rails of bigger ships.

tarp: (short for tarpaulin) a sheet, usually waterproofed canvas, spread over something to keep it dry

tiller: a handle attached to the rudder of a boat for steering

top sail: On a square-rigged ship, the sails directly above the mainsail. This would be the second sail above the deck.

transport: any ship used to haul soldiers or supplies

trim the sails: to adjust the sails on a boat or ship so as to make it sail properly

wharf: a place where ships dock

yankee jib: a small, high-cut jib

Yucatan: a peninsula of land, now part of Mexico, which lies due south of Galveston at the entrance to the Caribbean sea